Three for Three:
A Trio of Friendly MMF Ménage Tales

Stories of Friendship, Love, Sex... and Where They
Intersect

by
K. D. West

Stillpoint/Eros

Print ISBN: 978-1-938808-17-3
Ebook ISBN: 978-1-938808-15-9

K.D. West's Friendly Ménage tales:

Also in print from Stillpoint/Eros:
Four Erotic Tales: Letters to Allison

Contents

Truth & Games

Playing a Kids' Game... Adult-Style

"Let's play a game," Felicity said, as Aaron mixed their third round of Margaritas on her kitchen counter. Though it was late spring, it looked like anything but. The rain was coming down in sheets outside. Sheets.

Ben snorted. "What kind of game? Poker? You hate it. Go Fish?"

Felicity pulled one of her curls out so that she could see it, searching for the grey that would appear one of these years. "I had something different in mind," she said.

"What?" Aaron said wryly as he splashed tequila liberally into the pitcher, "Spin the Bottle? Truth or Dare?"

"Something a little more like that, I suppose," said Felicity as demurely as she could manage, reaching down and pulling a tiny clear vial from her purse, which was resting on the floor beneath the table.

"What the hell's that, Lici?" Ben asked. Aaron placed the lime-green pitcher in the center of table and peered at the little bottle, clearly intrigued.

"Truth serum," said Felicity and held up the label. "Amobarbital."

They stared at her. "Felicity," Aaron said, "Isn't that stuff supposed to be strictly controlled...?"

"I do have prescription privileges, you know. Besides, one of the perks of working in a research hospital," said Felicity. "I get to... circumvent some of the control laws from time to time."

"Fuck," Ben muttered. "I always said we were a bad influence on this girl."

She gave them what she hoped was a suitably evil smile.

"So," Aaron said, pouring the drinks out even as his eyes remained fixed on the bottle in Felicity's fingers, "what sort of game was it that you had in mind?"

"Well, first we drink up," Felicity said, carefully titrating three drops into each of the three glasses. Aaron was chewing his lip. Ben looked white as a sheet. "Don't you trust me?" she asked, and downed half of her sour-sweet tumbler.

"Course we do..." Ben muttered and looked to Aaron, who merely shrugged. "Fuck. Cheers."

"Cheers," Aaron said, and they drank, deeply.

As the Margarita hit bottom, Ben gave a shiver, then looked up. "So..."

Both men looked at her expectantly.

"What I have in mind is quite simple. Each of us gets to ask the other two a question — any question, and it has to be the same question for both people. And obviously," she said, raising her drink, "we have to answer honestly."

"Does the person who asks have to answer too?" Ben asked, his fingers drumming on the glass.

"Absolutely," Felicity said, and waited.

Aaron had his serious face on, and Ben's forehead was glistening with a thin sheen of sweat.

"Right," Aaron said, "I'll ask first."

Ben turned to look at his friend as though waiting to be attacked at any moment.

"Okay. Here it is: What's the wildest sexual experience you've ever had?"

Ben let out a bark of either agony or relief.

Felicity found herself talking. "Remember Lisa's bachlorette party? Maybe you don't, you were both out getting poor Connor shit-faced, if I remember. Anyway —"

"Don't tell me you slept with a male stripper!" Ben said, looking thoroughly disapproving.

"No, silly boy, it was your sister. Lisa was really drunk, and after everyone left, I was trying to help her get into my bed, just in the other room there —" Felicity pointed over her shoulder. "— so she could actually make it to her own wedding, when she reaches up and kisses me." In spite of everything, Felicity could feel the heat coming to her cheeks. "It was really weird. I mean, here's my best friend, other than you two, and she was doing things with her tongue that were just —"

"I DON'T WANT TO KNOW!" Ben shouted.

"And when I started to stick my fingers —"

"STOP!"

Ben and Aaron stared down at the drinks. "That stuff is amazing," Aaron muttered.

Ben grunted, looking even paler.

"I think I'm going to go into your bedroom and jack off right there on the bed," Aaron said. "That's the sexiest fucking thing I've ever heard."

"I think I'm going to be sick," Ben said.

"Really?" Felicity asked Aaron, ignoring Ben.

Aaron nodded. "Should I?"

"No," Felicity said, "I want to hear Ben's answer. Ben?"

Ben looked up at her, his face still white. "It was when we went to Anguilla after you finished med school, Lici. A Japanese girl, couldn't understand a thing she said, but it didn't matter. There was this hammock set up right on the beach, and we spent the entire night fucking without once touching the ground. Okay?" he whined.

"Uh, yeah," Aaron said. "Amazing. Let's see. Mine —"

"I don't want to hear it if it was Lisa, okay?" said Ben.

"But she took me up into the attic at your folks' house, Ben —"

"STOP, PLEASE!"

Aaron leaned over to Felicity and whispered, "She really could do the most amazing things with her mouth, couldn't she?"

Felicity began to giggle, until she saw Ben's miserable face. "Sorry," she said.

"No, you're not," Ben pouted.

"No, you're right, I'm not. You should see your face, Ben. You look absolutely mortified."

"Well, I am. It was bad enough knowing that Aaron used to sleep with my sister. But both of you?" He shook himself like a dog getting out of water, and Aaron and Felicity laughed. "I'll never use that bed in the attic ever again. And I'll never be able to look my sister in the face again."

Felicity began, "It was just the one —"

"STOP," Ben said, very firmly, and Felicity sat, her lips pursed, hands folded on the table before her.

"So," she said, once the urge to giggle had subsided again, "what's your question for us, Ben? I could tell you some things about Seamus... and Scott..." Ben and Lisa's younger brothers, who were also twins.

"Holy fucking hell, woman, is there a member of my family you haven't slept with?"

"Well," she said with a snort, her stomach warming in spite of the cold drinks, "at least it wasn't both of them at the same time. And of course, I've never slept with you." Both their faces contorted, Ben's in deep abashment and Aaron's in a sort of distracted thoughtfulness. "So," she repeated, "what do you want to ask us, Ben?"

"No sexual exploits, thanks a lot. I'll be digesting all of that for years." Some of the old fire flared back into Ben's eyes, making Felicity very warm inside indeed. "Okay, how about this: what's your happiest memory of school?"

They'd met in college, living on the same freshman dorm hallway.

"Wow," Aaron said, tapping the half-empty glass vial against the table, "I'll tell you the truth—choosing one is hard. There's the day we graduated. Couldn't believe we'd survived. Together. Then... Making the traveling squad for the track team. The first few months with Lisa — sorry, Ben," he said. Aaron's on-again-off-again romance with Ben's twin, which had ended finally when Lisa got engaged to their friend Connor, was the longest-standing relationship any of the three of them had had, in college or since. Felicity was happy that the Aaron and Lisa were friends again.

Aaron looked up at the ceiling. "There was a spring day during our senior year, right after I'd won my last race, when I remember just sitting down by the lake with you two, and Lisa and Seamus and Connor."

Ben nodded. Felicity could still smell the cool mossiness of the lake, the spicy scent of the eucalyptus floating across from the other side, the musk of Aaron's sweat. Ben playing his guitar.

"But really," Aaron said, "if I had to pick one, it would be junior year, after Lisa and I broke up the first time. I mean," he smirked, "me and Lisa fighting wasn't fun, but that isn't what I remember. It was after I got spiked at the UCLA meet, and you finally talking to me, Ben. And then you starting to cry, Felicity. And hugging us both. I thought you'd both gone absolutely nuts." He looked at them, his blue eyes flashing. "But I don't think I've ever been happier in my life."

Ben looked up, smiled, and punched Aaron in the shoulder, "Thanks, dude."

"Wow," Felicity murmured. "I was so happy then too. Even if I was crying and you didn't know what to do with me. And Alexei kissing me on the quad, though that doesn't seem like such a happy memory these days. Graduation, yes." Passing bottles of Cold Duck and Dom Perignon back and forth. "Meeting the two of you."

"Meeting us?" Ben crowed. "You came in and asked us what the hell we were doing in your room!"

Felicity blushed. She had miscounted the doors and was astonished to find that her roommates were apparently two boys: tall, fair Ben and wiry, dark Aaron.

Smirking, Aaron pushed her foot with his. "You all but told us we were useless idiots."

Blushing on, she laughed. "Well, you are useless idiots. But you were also the most beautiful boys I'd ever seen. Wish I'd stayed in your room. Connor wouldn't have minded rooming with Lisa and Jenn."

"God, Felicity," Aaron said, wrinkling his nose, "were you even seventeen yet? You'd never even had a boyfriend or anything, had you?"

She'd always been the youngest of them, though it'd never felt that way. "Well, no. But it's the truth," she replied, lifting her glass. Part of why she'd been so hard on them was that her first reaction to seeing two boys unpacking in what she was certain was her room had been very physical, very positive, and absolutely humiliating. "But the happiest memory? I mean, the happiest memory? It was later freshman year, Halloween. I'd wanted so much for you to like me, both of you, and you'd said all those horrible things about me, Ben — and yes, they were mostly true — but then Rick got me drunk, and the two of you…" Tears began to well up in her eyes. "Sorry. You backed him off, and stayed with me all night while I was throwing up, even though I knew you didn't like me very much…"

"We did like you," Aaron said, "sort of. We just hadn't realized it. And we didn't know what to do with you."

"We still don't," muttered Ben.

Felicity laughed. "It made me realize just who you two were. Not just that you were beautiful. That you were so wonderful, both of you. And so sweet. And funny."

"Funny looking, you mean," chuckled Ben, uncomfortable with sentiment as always.

Felicity shot him a look. "You came and took care of me because it was the right thing to do. That totally changed me."

"Did, didn't it?" Ben mused. He looked up. "You know, sometimes, I miss the old smartypants —" This time it was Felicity's turn to punch, and she landed a solid blow to his bicep. "Ow! I'm going to need that arm!"

Felicity smirked. "Good thing there's a doctor in the house then."

"Your turn, Ben. What's your happiest memory?" Aaron said quietly, swirling his glass.

"Till a few years ago," Ben said, rubbing his arm, "I would have said it was getting together with Maya. But the pleasure's faded right out of that." He'd pined after Maya for years. Sweet idiot. Ben shook his head and looked at Aaron. "Same as yours, dude. It'd been so hard being angry with you, hanging out with Seamus and Lisa. And being so angry that you'd gone and broken my sister's heart — and yeah, I know she was the one who called it off that time, that she hurt you, but it didn't feel it then. Mad that Her Majesty here wouldn't just take my side. Then watching you bleeding there on the track, and Lici and me climbing into each other's skins, we were so worried. And then it all just didn't matter any more, because you were all right, and you were talking to me again. And," he thrust a thumb towards Felicity, "she went fucking crazy and started weeping all over the two of us." He screwed up his face. "Funny thing to be happy about, you know?"

Aaron nodded, a smile barely painting his mouth. Then he turned back to Felicity. "So, Felicity, your turn. What's your question?"

She felt her stomach flutter. "Well." She looked from one to another, brown eyes and blue eyes focused on her. "The thing is..." But the fluttering bubbled right up into her throat and she couldn't speak. Damn. She was always better at theory than practice.

"Come on, Lici-lick-it," Ben said. "cough it up."

"You must have had a question you wanted to ask, or you wouldn't have dreamed this whole thing up," Aaron said, his gaze like the ocean off the Santa Monica pier that really calm day when Dad had bought her cherry soda, with sugar and everything. "Felicity. What's your question?"

"Ifyoucouldmarryanyonewhowoulditbe?" The words got out between the flutters, leaving her deflated.

Without a pause, without looking at each other, without blinking, both men answered, "You."

"Hunh."

"That's what I love about Felicity," Ben said. "She's so fucking articulate."

Twin tidal waves seemed to be sloshing up to her throat and down towards the pit of her stomach. Rebounding. Crossing. Rebounding again.

Aaron turned to Ben. "That's why I never could ask her out, you know? Because you..."

Ben nodded, then looked across the table. "C'mon, Felicity." Ben searched her face, very seriously. "Time for you to answer."

"Cards-on-the-table time." Aaron started to reach across to take her hand, but stopped himself. She stared at a point immediately between the two of them. "Felicity, if you could marry anyone in the world, who would it be?"

"You," she sighed to that point on the table. "Both of you. I've loved you both for as long as I've known you. I've wanted you both for... Well, for a very long time." She looked up. "I'd sort of hoped that one or both of you would admit that you have someone else you wanted to spend the rest of your life with. That I'd be spared the impossible task of choosing...."

Felicity stood, teetering — realizing just how drunk and nervous she was. "When I... dreamed this up, I knew you both might answer, you know, the way you did. It seemed so unlikely… But, in my, you know, in my fantasy, at this point…" She took a deep breath, squared her shoulders and looked at the two of them looking up at her. "I'm going right in there, into my bedroom. And I'm going to take off my clothes. And I am going to get into bed." She took another deep breath. "You are both welcome to join me. But only if it's both of you. If one or both of you finds this too… uncomfortable, I will certainly understand. Please lock the door on your way out, and we can pretend this never happened."

With as much dignity as she could muster, she stutter-stepped into her room and closed the door.

When she had fantasized this scene, she had been perfectly in control of her feelings, had treated them to a sultry retreat and a wink. Now however she was so terrified by what she had just said to them that she couldn't open the buttons to her blouse. She stood, fumbling with her own clothes, and cursing.

A low roll of thunder made the hair on Felicity's arms stand on end.

The door opened.

Aaron came in first, followed by Ben, who seemed to be trying to hide behind his friend, and was failing miserably, because of his height.

They were both entirely naked.

"Hunh."

"You said that before, Felicity." Aaron stepped to the side, looking perfectly relaxed, like Michaelangelo's David, except that he wasn't holding a sling and, oh, God, his very hard cock was pointed very emphatically just over Felicity's head. Also, unlike David, Aaron was demonstrably Jewish. He glanced to his side, where Ben was standing, slowly hyperventilating, his long hands over his crotch. "Ben, what are you doing? I've seen you naked before."

"She hasn't," Ben said. With a shamed smirk, he drew away his hands. A long arc of dark pink flesh was poking him in the navel.

Felicity couldn't even manage Hunh.

"So," Ben said, sidling away from Aaron. "Need help with that shirt?"

"Not yet," Felicity blurted, finding her articulators at last. "Just…

watch." It wasn't much of a strip show. It wasn't intended to be. She simply needed to find her feet again. Let the oxygen reach her brain again.

Aaron and Ben watched, very attentively.

Deliberately, methodically, she finally undid her blouse and dropped it from her shoulders. The boys stared fixedly at her bra. Well, at what was under the bra, Felicity supposed. Which was gratifying. She was happy that she had given in to impulse and gone for red lace instead of her usual white cotton — she could hear her mother tsking, Such a fuss to clean, Felicity, dear.

The bra followed the blouse to the floor. She could pick them up later. Skirt and panties dropped, and she could feel how wet she was, and how open, and Aaron actually whimpered, standing there.

"So," Ben said, so quietly that his voice almost faded into the sound of the rain against the window, "how are we going to, uh, do this?"

Felicity backed against her bed and sat on the big feather duvet. Reaching for two books on her bedside table, trying to keep the flutters from choking her again, she said, "I've been doing some research —"

Aaron and Ben burst into laughter and leapt onto the bed on either side of her.

Felix, the big black tom cat who had been her only long-term bedmate, yowled his disapproval and strutted out from behind Felicity's mound of pillows with a look of utter disdain on his feline face. Swishing his tail, he withdrew to the kitchen.

Her arms around either neck, Felicity gazed up at her two men. Who to kiss first?

With a strength she didn't know she had, she pressed the two faces together, and then pushed her lips against two open, astonished mouths. For a second, they both pulled against her, but the heat of the kiss pulled them both in, and their hands began to rove, both finding her flowing, flowering vulva at the same magical moment. Someone was groaning. Perhaps it was she.

Lightning flashed. Thunder rumbled.

Aaron broke first, but it was just to stare down at them. His eyes were so deep, and Ben's oak brown and full of flame. Aaron was sea and sky, that was it, and Ben was earth and fire. And that made her...

"I'm the quintessence," she sighed giddily. At least she thought she did, because at that moment, two tongues began to search her breasts, and all ability to speak was gone, and the old question of why humans have two nipples when one will do was answered in Felicity's mind forever.

For the rest of her life, Felicity would remember that night as an ecstatic blur punctuated by moments of arc-lit, lightning-struck clarity.

The first image — and Felicity was sure that it was the first, because her comforter was still on her bed — was of her thighs splayed over two sets of shoulders, two shocks of hair spraying onto her stomach, and the feeling of two tongues dancing like flame along her open sex. She was sure she was howling, but had no idea what words were coming out of her mouth.

But she could remember the taste of tears in her mouth, sharp and joyous.

The next memory — and Ben was fond of pointing out that he didn't believe that it was actually next, just the one that she and Aaron remembered as next — was lowering herself onto Aaron, feeling the thickness of him swell within her, feeling herself just on the edge of falling into those bottomless eyes. Aaron reaching up and caressing her cheek, nudging it slightly. She turned her head, mouth open, expecting to find Ben's tusk of a penis. Instead it was Ben's lips that met her, and she kissed him. And it was into his eyes that she gazed and into his mouth that she moaned when her cunt pulsed around Aaron's cock.

The image after that — and Ben of course insisted that it had happened first — was of the two boys sitting against her headboard, each stroking his own cock.

What a waste, she thought. "If one of you makes the other come, he can do anything to me that he wants."

Ben looked dubiously down at Aaron's cock, while Aaron pondered Felicity. "Anything?" Aaron asked.

"Anything," repeated Felicity, opening her legs wide just to emphasize the point.

She knew them well enough to know that they'd do just about anything if it involved friendly competition. What she hadn't expected was how comfortably they reached across and began to stroke each other.

Excited by the spectacle of these two beautiful men — her two beautiful men — happily wanking each other, and unwilling to make it easy on them, Felicity began to slip her middle finger inside herself, and to diddle her swollen clitoris with her thumb.

They both closed their eyes when she slid a second finger in. "Fuck, Lici, have a heart," Ben moaned.

"You two done this before?" Felicity teased.

"Uh," Aaron said. Ben turned scarlet.

"Really?" Felicity squealed, her thumb whirring faster.

"It was just um... once," Aaron panted, a look of intense concentration on his face. "Sophomore year. On Connor's bed. Drunk and horny as all fuck. All... four of us. Seamus. Connor!"

As Aaron had been talking, Ben had swooped down and gulped Aaron's bulbous cockhead into his mouth.

"Shit!" Aaron howled, eyes wide open, as he let go of Ben's penis and grabbed his friend's blond mane. Ben had sucked Aaron into his mouth all of three times before Aaron was screaming again, "Shit, Ben! Oh, God, shit!"

Felicity screamed too, her cunt pulsing around her fingers.

When Ben looked up, he had a triumphant gleam in his eye, and semen sprayed across most of his face. Felicity dove over to him and began cleaning his chin with her tongue. "Can't believe I did that," he said. "Hey, dude, you tell anyone I did that, and I'll tell 'em you enjoyed it!"

The taste of Aaron still bitter and slick on his lips, his tongue, Ben began to kiss Felicity passionately, so that she was fairly certain that Ben didn't hear Aaron say, "I did, actually."

"So," Felicity whispered into Ben's ear, "a deal's a deal. I'm all yours. What do you want?" She could imagine dozens of possibilities that he might suggest, most of which might be great fun, any of which she was actually willing to try in that moment.

His breath heavy in her ear, Ben panted, "I just want to fuck you, Lici. I've wanted to do that for so long..."

And so she lay back on the bed, and wrapped her legs up over Ben's hips while Aaron smiled, winked, and began to play with himself again.

The look on Ben's face would have made Felicity laugh if it hadn't melted her insides at the same time. He was so sweet and so hungry....

He sawed his long, curved prick slowly into her, sending sparks up to the crown of her head. His knees pressed under her hips and they began to roll rhythmically, gently, steadily, his teeth pulling at her neck, her nails pulling at his ass. Floating among the sparks in her brain was the realization that this was why they called it Rock and Roll, and that made her smile.

Somewhere, somehow — how did his head get in there? — Aaron's tongue began swirling around her labia and Ben's balls, which set them both off like Fourth of July rockets.

The rest of the night would become disjoined in her memory, an unplayed puzzle. Her teeth on someone's testicles — Aaron's, most likely. A finger circling her asshole, making her jump and laugh. A tongue passing an oyster-cool dollop of cum onto hers. Passing it along to a different tongue. The candles that she had lit at the four corners of her bed painting everything golden as memory.

She had spent a lifetime hating her body. Her breasts. Her thighs. Her hair. Yet Aaron and Ben adored her. They literally bathed her in desire and love and she felt so beautiful it hurt.

The last clear image — and she knows it is the last, because the storm had passed and tired morning light was leaking in through the window — was of Ben, flat on his stomach, one hand curled cozy around Aaron's cock, the other resting on Felicity's breast. "Got a new happiest memory," he muttered. "New wildest experience, too. Love you." And then he let loose a long, rasping snore.

"Love you," Aaron sighed. He was gazing down at Ben but running his big toe along Felicity's exhausted cunt lips in a way that would have been quite exciting had they been less sore, had she been less tired. As it was, the sensation was just lovely.

"Love you," Felicity sputtered out through sudden, heaving sobs. Aaron climbed up and wrapped her in his whip-tight arms and she sobbed more deeply still. Ben, sleeping, nuzzled her armpit comfortingly. "God! Aaron," Felicity whispered, "how is this going to work?"

"Felicity, lucky lady, we have walked through the Valley of the

Shadow of Death together. We came out together. We'll manage together now." Softly, he kissed her brow.

"Much better than you used to be with blubbering women," Felicity cried against his shoulder.

Aaron laughed. "Had more practice, I suppose. Felicity, if I ask you a question, will you tell me the truth?"

"Of course," Felicity said, feeling sleep begin to take her.

"It wasn't really truth serum, was it?"

"No," she snuffled. Mixing barbiturates and alcohol could be lethal. And really, there was no such thing as truth serum. "Rose water. Does it matter?"

"Nope," Aaron said. "Still want to hear about you and Lisa some time."

She smiled, feeling warmer than anyone ever had a right to feel on a raw spring morning. Felix sauntered back in, apparently assured that his rest would be disturbed no further, and curled himself above Felicity's pillow.

And then Aaron pulled the duvet back over them all and they drifted into sleep.

Epilogue: Verity

Truth... and Consequences

It was infuriating, it truly was. Since Lisa had confirmed that the baby was definitely a girl, the boys had committed the unpardonable sin not once but three times: they'd awoken a last-trimester Felicity with their bickering.

Infuriating was hardly the word for it.

They had been fighting over the name the last time. Strictly speaking, Aaron hadn't been fighting, he had been sulking. In typical Aaron fashion, he had announced that he thought it would be appropriate that their child be named after his late mother, Eva, and had left it at that — well, that, and broadcasting loud silence whenever another possibility was mentioned. Aaron, the orphan. Their Richie Rich.

It had been Ben who had done most of the bickering, Ben the twin who came from an enormous family. He had insisted that they should name the baby after his mother, who, they were astonished to discover, was actually named Boudicca.

Felicity had been so depressed by the battle that she had been unwilling to enter the fray and suggest her own beloved grandmother's name: Verity. She had merely told them both that they were being childish, morbid… and obscenely inconsiderate, given how hard it was for her to sleep in her distended state.

They'd all agreed, finally, that the last name should be Harris-Marcovitz — Ben and Aaron's last names, hyphenated. As Felicity had patiently explained, no one would ever question who the child's mother was. Given the unconventional domestic arrangement, it seemed sensible to make Ben and Aaron's joint fatherhood very clear. But they'd never settled on a first name, and Felicity despaired of coming to any kind of consensus.

This evening, awakened for the fourth time, Felicity tried hard to get back to sleep, but it was impossible. Aaron was the one doing the insisting, and his voice had a desperate undertone to it that set Felicity's teeth on edge, even as it broke her heart. That, and mild contractions where reminding her of pain soon to come.

"Have a heart, Ben. You're surrounded by people who are yours. You've always had a family. The only relatives I've ever known were some distant cousins and my mom's lawyer, who doesn't exactly count. Can you blame me for hoping she comes out with black hair and brown eyes?"

"Dude," Ben wheedled, "everything you've ever had has been yours. I know it's hard, but your life is full of one-of-kind this and unique that. I've had to share fucking everything — even you with Lici and Lici with you. I just want a child that I know is mine."

"I've always shared you and Felicity," Aaron sighed.

Ben sighed, an octave lower. "Maybe it'll be a red-head — that could be either one of us."

"Nah," Aaron muttered. "Linked gene — remember what Lici said? If my mum had passed red on to me, I'd have come out auburn or dark brown, not black-haired."

"Well," Felicity said, as tartly as she could manage, rolling over and staring down at them, where they were sitting against the bottom posts of the bed, "I'm glad one of you actually listened to something I said, even if it wasn't the bit about not waking me, or the bit about never calling me that fucking name — "

They both gaped at her, clearly deeply sorry that they'd disturbed her sleep. Then they both looked at each other and smiled. "But Lici…"

She growled and tried to sit up — not an easy task when you're carrying an extra forty pounds. "Look, you two, you know I only put up with it from Alexei because he couldn't handle anything more than two syllables at a time. Now if one of my child's fathers isn't able to do better than that — "

They both laughed, and climbed up the bed to either side of her, kissing her as they came.

"That's more like it," she said, trying to sound just as arch, trying not to sound as if she were about to giggle. "In the first place, the two of you know perfectly well we have no way of knowing whose sperm it actually was." That night was a bit of a blur for all three of them. "In the second place, what difference does it really make? And in the third place, I'm tired, you've woken me, and I expect the two of you to make me comfy."

Hands began to grope.

"No, not that way, you adolescent nitwits." Felicity did giggle, finally, even as her annoyance blossomed. "Yes, I know, it's supposed to encourage the softening of the cervix, but I told you, I'm tired, and I have no interest in rewarding the two of you for waking me."

The hands continued to explore, and lips.

"Oh, fine." She pushed down on both of them, lifting herself laboriously up and climbing out of the bed. "I'm going to take a bath. I've got some nasty psychoactives that I will happily use on whichever reprobate..." An implosion of pain sucked her in. It felt as if every muscle in her lower body was attempting to pull itself loose from her skeleton all at once. "Oh, FUCK!" she howled.

When awareness returned, it brought a sweet smell, the sight of both boys gaping at her in concern, the trickle of some fluid down her legs, and the sound of her own disembodied voice saying, "I think it's time to call Lisa, don't you?"

Some fifteen hours later, Felicity was in bed again — a different bed — a baby happily attempting to nurse, Lisa gingerly attempting to heal some of the damage occasioned by the baby's arrival, and a feeling of exhausted fulfillment suffusing her weary, untethered body.

Their faces glowing with awe and a kind of fear she had never seen in them, not even during the years when they were risking their lives on a regular basis just for fun, the boys were whispering again, at the foot of the hospital bed. This time the conversation involved a lot of mutual nodding, and so she happily left them to it.

"How you doing?" asked Lisa as she gently cleaned Felicity off.

"Wonderful," sighed Felicity. "Hurts, but it feels wonderful."

Lisa smiled. "Sort of like losing your virginity, only a thousand times more so."

"Hmmm. That's just about right.... I do feel a kind of like a sail someone's forgotten to pull in...."

Laughing, Lisa finished her exam. "Yeah, that'll get better. I'd better move up there," the doctor said, looking around at her twin brother and Aaron, who were still deep in conversation. "If I keep playing around between your legs, Ben's going to start turning green soon."

"Keep playing around between my legs, and you're going to make Aaron very happy," Felicity joked, surprised she had it in her.

"Well," Lisa said with a smirk, "we can't have that. Especially as poor Connor would be broken-hearted to have missed it."

"Hmmm." Felicity was focused down at the baby. Wheat hair, cornflower eyes. "Connor?"

Lisa prodded at Felicity's exposed breast. "Oh, good, you're expressing collostrum... My lovely husband and our lovely sons are out in the waiting room with the rest of the horde. Mmm. You should be letting down properly in the next few days..."

"Horde?" Felicity asked, fatigue pulling at her.

Lisa's face twisted into a bemused smile as she backed up and removed her no-longer white robes. "These two were taking turns helping you and making calls." She turned to Aaron and Ben. "I can probably hold them off for another twenty minutes. You might want to get to know your new daughter."

The boys looked up at Lisa and — without even getting up — pulled her into a stifling hug.

"Thanks, sis," Ben said.

Lisa turned a deep red, muttered, "You're welcome," and tried to extricate herself.

Once her friend had fought free, Felicity looked down to where her child's fathers were sitting, looks of unaccustomed solemnity on their faces. "Calls?" she asked.

The serious expressions melted to sheepishness — one Felicity was much more familiar with. Ben murmured, "Well, I contacted my family..."

"And I called your folks. And. One or two others. Friends and such," Aaron said.

Lisa laughed. "Both sets of grandparents have been out there for hours. They're positively vibrating. Seamus and Scott are there — watch the stuffed animals, you wouldn't believe what they put in some of the ones they gave Billy. A couple of your lab friends, whose names I can never remember. Uncle Harry's passing around a flask of bourbon. Oh, and just about everyone wanted to know if you needed help with a name."

Ben moaned. Aaron said, "No, we don't need help."

Lisa laughed again, and so did Felicity, shaking the nipple out of the baby's mouth, which set her thinly wailing. "Well," Lisa said, once Felicity had settled her back on the breast, "I'd better go try and keep the natives from becoming too restless. See you lot in a bit," Lisa said as she left the room.

Ben and Aaron seemed to have rematerialized on either side of the bed, looking at the baby so adoringly that what was left of Felicity's middle started to melt.

"She's...." Aaron looked for the word and failed.

"Beautiful," Ben supplied, and it was a judgment they both seemed content with.

Felicity found tears dripping down from her nose onto the fine fair hair. "I was blonde till I was three or so," she said, looking up at them, "and Caucasian babies often start with blue eyes...."

"Doesn't matter," Ben sighed.

"Not at all," Aaron agreed.

Felicity cried some more.

"And about the name," Aaron said. "We were thinking, maybe..."

The two of them looked to each other, then to her. Together they said, "Lici?"

When Felicity's jaw dropped, they both laughed. "Sorry," Aaron said. "Just kidding."

Ben ran his fingers through the baby's hair. "Actually, we wanted to ask you something." He looked up to Aaron.

"We were actually thinking," Aaron said, resting a finger on the infant's cheek, still stained by birth, "of asking you what you might think...." He looked into her eyes, then up at Ben.

"Given how this all started with a game of Truth and Dare... We wondered if you'd thought of naming her after your grandmother."

Felicity looked down at the miniscule miracle that was snoring at her incredibly sore breast. "Verity," she said, tears flowing again.

The Visitor

A Tale of Embracing the Unknown... Literally

Lea didn't usually masturbate in airplane bathrooms, because, after all, they're bathrooms. On airplanes.

But half of the way through the long flight across the country to Atlanta, she found herself in the tiny, tinny cubicle with one foot up on the wall and the other in the sink, with her fingers buried to the second knuckle in her pussy.

Thinking of Sean, her best friend's older brother.

Sean the firefighter of the broad shoulders and the narrow hips. Sean of the gentle Southern drawl, the polite tone, the blue eyes, and the wicked, square-jawed smile.

Sean, who she had always wanted to wrap her arms and legs around, but never managed to do more than flirt with a bit.

Sean. Who had found out that she was interviewing for the job in Atlanta and had, with smooth, apparently subtext-less Southern hospitality, invited her to save the cost of a hotel room and stay with him. Well, on the sofa of the apartment he shared. But still. Just a door away... Oooo, Sean.

She wanted him. She had always wanted him, since she was a college sophomore and his sister Kirsten's roomie. She wanted his strong arms around her. Wanted his big hands pulling her pelvis tight against his. Wanted to feel what she knew would be his big, thick cock spreading... Ooo...!

With a shudder of pleasure and relief that she knew was only temporary, she came, swallowing as best she could the groan that wanted to explode from her gut.

Carefully, quickly, Lea lowered her legs, pulled up her panties, pulled down her skirt and smoothed it as best she could, washed her hands, and opened the bathroom door.

A woman just a few years older than Lea stood in the narrow galley glaring daggers at her. Her elbow-high child was doing a dance that made unmistakably clear just how long they'd had to wait.

"Sorry," Lea murmured. "Thanks."

"Yaw're welcome," the mother grumbled in a thick-as-honey accent that made Lea feel anything but welcome as the woman and her child pushed past.

Even so, hearing that Southern sound got Lea thinking of Sean again, of his arms and chest and ass and mouth... and got her wondering just how long the mom and kid were going to take, because, oh, she could have started all over, airplane bathroom or no.

The plane finally landed and Lea picked up the beat-up old Civic she'd rented. Sean had told her that he'd have loved to pick her up, but he wasn't going to be getting off duty until about the time Lea landed, and since she was going to need a car the next day anyway to get to the interview, she drove herself north from the airport — around the city and into Cobb County, where Sean and the other firefighter shared a place, where she'd be sleeping on their couch.

Well, she thought let's not lie: Lea hoped that she wouldn't be sleeping on their couch. She hoped very much that she would at last be sharing Sean's bed. She knew that she should have been thinking about the interview, but hey — there are lots of jobs. There was only one Sean, and she'd lusted after him for far too long.

Well. She was thinking about the job interview. It was for the position of assistant business manager of a mid-sized professional theater — her chance finally to work somewhere other than the glorified community theaters she'd been slaving at since graduation.

She was excited by the opportunity.

But Sean.…

Her thoughts less on the road than they should have been, she followed her phone's directions around the city, past dozens of malls, hotels, and office buildings mostly bearing the name Peachtree Whatever, and out into the gently rolling hills and lush greenery of the Atlanta suburbs. "Exit the highway," said her phone, and she exited. "Turn left," it intoned, and she turned left.

She wondered if she could give her GPS voice a Southern accent. Tuhn leyeft, honey. That thought made Lea smile.

She reached the complex, parked, and followed Sean's very clear directions to his second-floor apartment. Fighting down the images of Sean's broad chest — and narrow hips — that had driven her to the airplane lavatory, she knocked on the door.

A muffled voice called out, "C'me in! It's unlocked."

She opened the door and was assaulted simultaneously by the delicious smells of something sweet baking and something frying, as well as by the vision of the tall, tapered figure at the stove.

Him. Cooking. Looking like every masturbatory fantasy Lea had ever had about him, only better. Except fully dressed, but food. Shit.

"Sorry I couldn't come to the door," he said in that sweet Georgia drawl. He finished flipping something in the pan. "I'm up to my elbows in fried chicken. Hope you like — "

Lea threw her arms around him from behind and took joy in squeezing his chest hard. "I love it! Thank you so much for having me."

"Uh. Welcome." He stiffened before relaxing and turning in her grasp. "Nice to meet you, too, miss."

Lea looked up at the eyes smiling down at her. Brown. At the dimpled chin. Not Sean. Oh, SHIT. She released the man — he had to be Sean's roomie — and stammered, "I'm so, so… I, uh…"

"Naw, miss, don't be sorry, that was a nice hello, no doubt!" The roommate put down his tongs and smiled at her. He held out his enormous hand. "I'm Andrew. You must be Lea."

She shook his hand and nodded, still speechless.

His grin grew. "Really, don't feel bad. It happens more often than you'd think — the captain mixes us up so much he's taken to just calling us the Twins."

"Huh," Lea grunted. She was feeling the ghost of that muscled chest on her fingers.

"There you are, Lea!" Another Southern voice called from the other side of the apartment. She turned: it was Sean, no doubt this time. Blue eyes. Square jaw. Nothing on but a towel around his waist. Oh. Shitty shit-shit. He ran his hand through his short, wet hair. "Sorry, I was just taking a shower, I didn't want you to have to smell me like the hog I am."

"Huh," Lea repeated.

Sean smiled warmly. "I see you met Andy. I hope, Andy," he said, his voice lowering in mock threat, "that you've conducted yourself like a gentleman toward this young lady."

"I wasn't the one came out half-naked," joked Andy.

Lea found her voice. "Besides, I was the one molesting him."

Sean raised his eyebrow, that supremely wicked grin on display.

"Yeah," laughed Andy, "lucky me! She thought I was you. Couldn't see your ugly face 'cause I was dealing with supper."

"My ugly face!"

"Anyhow," Andy laughed, "why didn't you tell me our visitor was such a bombshell? Begging your pardon, Miss Lea."

Lea felt Sean's eyes flash to hers, saw the smile turn from wicked to evil. "Didn't want you getting ideas, Andy."

Lea couldn't think of anything to say to that.

"Ideas, huh?" Andy snorted and turned back to the stove. "You go get some pants on, boy, and we'll have some supper and then we can talk about who's getting ideas."

Now Sean's grin turned sunny again; he waved and turned, and Lea was treated to the sight of his retreating, naked, rippling back and his tight, towel-clad ass as they made their way down the hall.

I'm getting ideas, Lea thought, and then tried very hard not to think any more.

Dinner — supper — was of course fried chicken, with, of course, corn on the cob and amazing peach pie. "You've now hit all of the high points of Georgia cuisine," Sean joked.

"Hey!" said Andy, "we haven't even got to grits and boiled

peanuts!"

Making a face, Sean said, "What a shame."

"You call yourself a Georgia boy?" said Andy. "You're all city, Sean, admit it."

"You have to be from the country to be a Georgian?" Sean raised an eyebrow.

"Naturally," Andy replied. "Q.E.D."

Trying not to get totally lost in enjoying their banter (flirtation?), Lea said, "Sounds like something my mom always used to say: if you live in New York, you're Jewish. If you're Jewish living outside New York, you're goyisch. Um, gentile."

"Me," said Sean, "I have always considered myself a citizen of the world."

Andy laughed, "Yeah, listen to the cosmopolitan here. Visit's his sister off in California, and he comes back talking about artichokes and pizza with all kinds of fancy stuff on it, and sushi."

"I didn't know you liked sushi, Sean!" To be honest, Lea couldn't remember Sean ever eating a meal that he didn't seem to enjoy.

"Oh," Sean said, he eyes holding hers once more, "I love sushi." His tone barely changed, and his expression seemed to hold exactly the same open, welcoming grin, but there was something about the way he said it that made Lea's middle flutter as she imagined him kneeling between her legs. Imagined the feeling of his tongue... He winked.

He's flirting with me, Lea reveled. Oh, god, yes, he's flirting with me.

Andy laughed again and popped open another beer for Lea. "Now see, me, I like my fish too, but I like it as the first course, not the main dish."

Lea's eyes snapped to Andy's and she saw that he too had a lazy, sexy smile on, and that — yes — she hadn't imagined the sexual undertones this time either. Playing games, gentlemen? She took a swig of her cold beer and twirled the drumstick bone she'd been fiddling with. "Well," she said, letting her voice grow raspy, "I like my meat red, generally. Love to chew on a rib, for instance. Nice, long, hard rib, dripping juices down my chin..." She ran her tongue up the length of the bone. "Mmm." When both men's jaws dropped, she couldn't help it: she laughed.

Sean and Andy were both turning bright red, but they too laughed, long and hard.

"Mind," Lea finally managed to say, waving the bone, "this chicken really was fabulous."

"Thank you," Andy said with a smile and mock bow.

They proceeded to drink and talk. And drink some more. Beer. And then some bourbon. And then some more.

And Lea was flirting with two fantastically hot firemen, and they were both flirting back, and she felt absolutely fucking fabulous.

And just at the point that Lea was ready to pull her shirt off and yell, COME TO MAMA! to them both, Sean — or maybe it was Andy — stood up and reminded Lea that she had an interview in the morning. And then Andy — or maybe it was Sean — walked remarkably steadily over to the couch, pulled it out, and began to make up Lea's bed.

And the other helped.

For a brief moment, watching the two burly boys arranging her pillows and smoothing her sheets with an almost military precision, Lea indulged in an image of both of them stripping off their t-shirts, dropping their jeans and joining her....

But then both stepped away, wished her a good night, and sauntered together back toward where their bedrooms were. Each seemed to be trying to make sure that the other was leaving the room first, but eventually they left side by side, their shoulders barely clearing the hallway walls.

Well, shit.

As Lea slipped off her skirt, her shirt, her bra, and the panties that she'd been wanting to shed since she entered the apartment, she stood there, horny, naked, and more than a little drunk. I could sneak into Sean's bed, she thought. He wouldn't kick me out, I know it. Or Andy's. Or...

She shook her head. No. They'd made the sensible choice. She sat down and started to look for her pajamas....

But the air was warm and thick.

And she was tired. And light-headed.

And so she slipped, pajama-less, under the covers in the foldout bed, dreaming that the fingers stroking her clit and teasing her nipples belonged to two very large, very strong, very different sets of hands.

Lea's dream was very, very pleasant. In it, someone… Or perhaps more than one someone… Well. In either case, licking of her foot was involved, by a tongue or tongues unknown. Mmm.

Her eyes fluttered open.

It wasn't a dream.

A tongue was in fact running up Lea's instep, sending a flare to her crotch that caused her to writhe on her belly and groan. Mmm.

"Hey, Lea." The voice was soft and male and Southern. "Thought you might want some company."

Between the pleasant suddenness of her wakening and the alcohol that was still in her system, Lea could only manage a throaty "Uh-huh." She spread her legs wide, her foot pulling the sheet aside and uncovering her lower body.

"Mmm," whispered the voice. "I like peach pie just fine, but this was what I wanted for dessert."

"Uh… huh!"

Without warning the tongue had slid all of the way up her inner thigh and licked the entire length of her pussy, sending Lea's smoldering arousal into full flame.

"Shh." He chuckled. "Don't want to wake no one. 'Cept you, 'course."

Lea wanted to say something smart, but a whimper was the best she could do. Her pelvis arched up of its own accord.

Whichever of the men he was, he was clearly a gentleman. He took the invitation graciously and dove in. His tongue and lips began to tease and pleasure her lips and clit. His nose tickled her asshole, the hot breath sending what was already an indescribable sensation truly transcendent.

"Hnnnh!"

"Shh," he said again, this time against her clit.

Trembling, Lea stuffed her face into the pillow, screaming into it as he pleasured her with his tongue, his lips, his nose. When his fingers slid up under her belly and began to massage her breasts, she lost all sense of what was happening and where — her body was one nerve, pulsing, now.

Usually, Lea liked long, slow bouts of foreplay, liked kissing and touching and feeling a man slowly meander his way to going down on her. There was something wonderfully romantic about watching a head wandering down her belly and between her thighs. Nose bobbing as he lapped at her. Eyes open and smoldering or closed and abandoned as he pleasured her.

But this? Having her face shoved into the pillow, her ass up in the air, and that mouth.…. Even if Lea had been on her back, even if it had been less than pitch black, she didn't think that she'd have been able to see straight anyway.

Thick, strong fingers pulled and teased remarkably gently at her nipples, causing her to scream on into the pillow as wide, fine lips sucked her sizzling clit against a fluttering tongue. Cleft chin, or square? she found herself wondering for a moment, though of course his chin was down between her spread thighs where she couldn't tell. But then an electric spark began to shoot from her clit up her spine, joining with the arcs of pleasure fired by those amazing fingers in flaring up to her brain and shutting down all thought quite effectively.

Thunder rumbled. At first, Lea thought it was her imagination, part of the monumental orgasm that set her aflame. Then, as the explosion subsided, she realized that not all of the lightning was inside of her. There was a storm outside, the kind that rarely visited Lea's home state.

Her visitor was kissing his way from her right cheek of her ass across the dimple at the base of her spine to the left cheek.

"Fuck me," moaned Lea into the pillow. "Fuckmefuckme."

"Yes, ma'am," said the deep voice. "Always give a lady what she asks for, that's what I was always taught." She heard him fishing for something, heard the distinctive crinkle of a foil condom package being opened, a rubber being rolled down over a hard cock. A wide hand ran over her ass, her back, sending a tremor through Lea. . "Like this, or — ?"

"Fuck. Me." She reached back between her legs, found a hard, long, latex-encased penis, and pulled it toward her.

"Yes, ma'am," he said, a quaver of desire in his voice that made Lea feel incredibly sexy and incredibly hot and that made her want him inside of her right now.

Again: Lea usually preferred to face her lover — whether in straight missionary position or with a leg or two over his shoulders — for a couple of reasons. First of all, she liked being able to see the affect she had on a man, could be in itself an incredible turn on. Second, she liked the feeling of the cock plowing the front wall of her pussy. Lea had discovered her G-spot long before she'd ever heard the term, had discovered that, unlike most of her girlfriends, she could have a very satisfying orgasm just from being fucked (so long as her lover was big enough and lasted long enough).

Just now, however, she didn't mind being banged from behind, her face still stuffed into her pillow.

As this cock head pressed into Lea's pussy, however, she gasped in surprise, feeling it surge along the front wall of her vagina: this cock, unlike any she'd ever had inside of her, curved down.

It was perfect.

It made her scream. If there was thunder and lightning rolling on, Lea couldn't have seen or heard, because the cock that was now pounding hard into her sent her nerves roaring, her blood screaming.

Orgasm, which hadn't ever quite left her, came howling back, playing hide-and-seek with her consciousness as her visitor slammed into her, one massive paw pulling her hips back against him as the other reached around and found...

Found her clit, and...

Oh, FUCK.

Was she dreaming again? Was it all just one enormous, wet blurry wet....

Lea's fingers reached down her belly between her legs. No cock.

No cock, but fabulously tender. Wet.

Had she hallucinated it? Or had she passed out, drunk and spent on whiskey and sex?

Blearily she turned over, looking for...

Lightning flashed, revealing a broad-shouldered silhouette. "Fuck," he said. "You are so fucking beautiful."

So are you, Lea tried to say, but couldn't be sure that any intelligible sound had passed her lips. She reached up, her slick fingers finding a muscled chest, caressing a tiny, jewel-hard nipple.

"Shit." He hissed, and leaned forward, his lips finding hers as the retreating storm finally rumbled its own approval.

The flame inside of Lea, barely banked, flared back to light. Not quite so urgent as before, but no less strong, and so she pulled his body to hers, burying herself in him, running her finger along his ribs, the muscles of his back, feeling that hard cock, un-rubbered now, straining and leaking against the outside of her thigh.

Yet he seemed in no hurry this time, and so Lea was able to indulge and kiss and explore.

Her fingers counted the vertebrae down to the taut swell of his ass, the concave plane of his hips.

His fingers flowed slowly, reverentially over her flesh: her hips, her belly.

Down? Please?

Well, no: as they kissed, as their tongues danced, those amazing, enormous, shockingly delicate fingers explored upward, skirting the outside of one aching breast, defining the line of her collar bone, of her throat, her earlobe....

How was it that a light touch against her ear could make goose pimples erupt all of the way down to her knees? She moaned into his mouth; desire clutched her again, throbbing through her. She wanted him inside of her — wanted him so much — and yet...

And yet the passion of their last fuck and the languor of this session had left her without will, without a muscle in her body. She was his, to take at whatever pace it pleased him, and oooohhh, it pleased him to take his sweet, sweet, Georgia-peach time, and it pleased her to be taken so.

Lea had lost her virginity during the summer before her senior year of high school. She and Sam had been dating for two years at that point, and had done just about everything that could be done with fingers and mouths, and so Lea hadn't been shocked at Sam's urgency or his hair trigger. Not shocked, but disappointed. They'd eventually worked out how to make sure that she got her fair share out of their sessions: it had usually involved lots of kissing and caressing, ending with his head between her thighs. He hadn't been exactly patient, but he had at least tried, the sweetie. Of the dozen or so lovers she'd had since, the more successful had usually followed a similar formula:

petting her until she was worked up, getting her off with their tongues, then pumping into her until they got off. When she was really lucky, the man lasted long enough and was properly endowed — neither too well nor not well enough — so that the pressure of his cock against her G-spot and his pelvis against her clit got her off again before he exploded.

None of them had ever managed to set her alight without actually touching her crotch.

Her new lover was getting dangerously close. All with a slow, gentle touch that spread over her like honey on fire.

He broke their kiss, and Lea whimpered. And yet when the lips began a voyage along her chin to her ear, tongue flowing lightly around the lobe and in before continuing down her neck even as those amazing fingers began to outline the curves of her breasts, she found that she couldn't complain.

He kissed on down, licking at the hollow of her throat and at her chest, at the top of one swelling, aching breast, even as his fingers traced the bottom of her rib cage, the lines of the abs she never thought she had, the tightly trimmed bush of her pubes.

And at the same bright, shining moment, his lips closed around her right nipple as one of his hands caressed the other and the other hand slid over her pussy lips, stroking her vibrating clit.

Even in the moment, Lea was disappointed that she couldn't have enjoyed that slow, fabulous journey for longer. Even in the moment, Lea knew that she felt so fucking good.

Clenching her jaw, pressing her mouth against the top of his head, she screamed once again, her thighs clamping around his hand as a slow-motion tidal wave of an orgasm sloshed up through her and back down, leaving her limp and quivering.

She collapsed, her head flopping back, her legs falling apart, her eyes falling closed and her mouth falling wide open.

Holy fucking shit. Fuck. Oh, fuck.

How long had they been at it? Ten minutes? An hour? Long enough for the storm to have wandered away. Long enough for her to have come three times, each as hard as she could ever remember coming. And I don't even know which...

He kissed her breast lightly, his fingers still on the other nipple, his other hand still gently cupping her pussy. "God," he groaned, "you're so fucking wet."

"For you," she rasped. "You... fuck? Please."

"Oh, God, yes," he hissed, and Lea once again heard the sound of a hand fumbling in a pocket, of a foil packet being ripped.

This time she wanted to help roll the latex down over that magnificent erection, but her arms were boneless. She heard him grunt as he finished putting on the condom — next time, she'd have to invest in an IUD or a diaphragm or get back on The Pill — any fucking thing so they wouldn't have to wait....

Lea started to roll on her belly again, but he stopped her. "Naw," he sighed. "Wanna see you."

And so, half-conscious, she lay back as he slid between her legs, placing himself at her entrance. "Ready?" he grunted.

Lea nodded, or thought she did.

Whichever, he pressed himself in, filling Lea with airless, dark flame. "Fuck!" he moaned.

"Yup." Lea grinned. Felt her entire body grin.

As he slowly pressed in, stretching her wide once again, he leaned down and kissed her — no teasing this time, just lips on lips. Closing the circuit.

In close embrace, in full contact from nose to knee, they began to fuck. Fuck indeed!

Well, to be completely honest, she was still as limp as a rag doll. He was doing the fucking, slowly, with agonizing tenderness that was just as intoxicating as the wild abandon from earlier. She could feel flare of his cock pressing along the ripples of her vaginal walls, could feel...

Fuck.

As they fucked — as he fucked her — his hands continued to explore, to enrapture. She could feel him stoking the flickering flame of her arousal, could feel it building, but so, so slowly that it made her want to weep, even as it made her want to sing.

John, with whom she'd lived for almost a year before moving back in with Kirsten, had gotten off on tying Lea up, teasing her. Edging, he called it: keeping her on the verge of coming for as long as he could before finally giving her release — but only when she was begging for it. She'd gone along with this game because it felt fucking good, but it had turned out to be one of a number of clues that he was a controlling asshole. A pleasant clue, but still...

This slow, slow fuck didn't feel like Lea's lover was trying to control her. It simply felt as if he was in control, savoring the delight with her, as if they were sharing a particularly fabulous meal.

"You... feel so fucking... good," he moaned into Lea's mouth.

Once again, "Yup" was all that Lea could reply. Or possibly "Yum."

She could feel a slick layer of sweat beginning to form between them, could feel his nipples, small and tight, dragging against hers, could feel the blood build up around her G-spot as the fabulous, wonderful, unbelievable cock massaged it, gently but mercilessly. Could feel arousal expanding her infinitely outward.

"Legs," she panted, "up...."

He understood, apparently, because he slid his hands down under her knees and lifted them as he arched backward and pressed her calves up over his square shoulders. Opening her to him. All without stopping his thrusts.

The change in angle absolutely scrambled what was left of Lea's brain, as her body clearly had clearly known that it would. The fuck was the only thing that existed in the world. It was a universal fuck. A metaphysical fuck.

He was speeding up — minutely, but noticeably, he pistoned into her more quickly, more forcefully. Lea wanted to beg him not to come too soon, to wait for the avalanche that was bearing down on her to sweep her away.

But her lips wouldn't form words.

His thrusts began to become less and less measured, more and more frantic, and Lea almost wept, because it felt so fucking good, but she was so close and...

And as her demon lover gave one last gigantic, spastic thrust, he reached between them and pushed his wide thumb firmly but gently against her clit, pressing it against the base of his cock, and...

And the avalanche carried her off in a flood of white pleasure, and if she were never to wake again, she considered it a fair trade. Aloha. Shalom. Arrivaderci. Sayonara.

To her surprise, however, she didn't die.

"Oh, gawd, oh, gawd," her lover gasped, his chest heaving against hers. Her legs were bent nearly flat against her torso, a level of flexibility she'd never quite managed in yoga, but was reveling in now, because she could feel his cock still within her, still pulsing. Which caused her to contract around him. Which made them both call out to a higher power.

Carefully, still buried in her, he released her legs. With as much regret as relief, she lowered them, squeezing his softening erection out of her body, which made both of them moan at the loss.

Lea became aware that her back, her ass, her legs — they were all burning. She was going to be sore as all fuck the next day.

But it was worth it.

They lay there, still entangled, as their breaths and pulses slowed. They kissed again. No frenzy. Just touching.

She must have fallen asleep at some point, because she startled to find him tucking her under the covers.

"Shh," he said, and placed a feather-light kiss on her forehead. "You get some sleep, now, you hear?"

"'Night," she rasped.

But he was gone.

One last distant rumble of thunder shook the night.

And all was darkness.

When Lea's phone started crowing at her to wake up and greet the bright new day while the sky was still dark — while it was still the middle of the night back on the West Coast — she slapped at it with a groan. Fucking...

Fucking.

Thunder. And a mouth on my foot. And a nose against my asshole. And a cock screwing me into the pillow. Fingers like feathers of fire. A slow, full-body fuck for the ages.

Fucking...

Must have been a dream, right?

Lea shifted, trying to shake the cobwebs from her brain, and her body screamed at her that it had been no dream. She was sore from knees to nose, but it was a fabulous sore, better than anything she'd ever endured after a run or a yoga class.

Trying to sort out just what had happened from the swirling mass of over-amped sensory impressions, Lea rolled (somewhat tenderly) to the side of the pull-out mattress. *Amazing you're still standing.* She patted the sofa-sleeper on the arm-rest. *Well done!*

Grabbing toiletries and her bathrobe, she made her way to the bathroom.

Which was right between the two firemen's bedrooms.

Which one was it? She couldn't decide whether she wanted her phantom lover to have been the man she'd had a crush on since she was nineteen or the stranger she'd just met.

Either way, they were both snoring, clearly sound asleep.

One of them had truly earned it, that was for sure.

Smiling — still moving gingerly — she went into the bathroom, closed the door somewhat regretfully, and took a long, hot shower that almost returned her body to her.

When she wrapped herself in her light silk robe and stepped out of the steamy bathroom, she was greeted by two very solemn looking, bare-chested boys.

"Morning, Miss Lea," Andy said, while Sean simply turned "Lea" into an eight-syllable twelve-bar-blues of a mumble.

"Good morning, gentlemen!" she chirped, thinking, *One of you was the best fuck I have ever had in my life, and I have no idea which of you it was.*

"What do y'all want for breakfast?" mumbled Andy.

Sean muttered back, "You made supper, Andy. I'll take care of this one."

Each of them had his eyes on her, but even so, both of them seemed more aware of each other than of her.

Oh, god, she groaned inwardly, *they're both trying to mark their territory.* And while the idea held a certain amount of abstract fascination, she had absolutely no interest in being fought over or peed on. "It seems to me, gentlemen," she said, aiming for sweet-and-unassailable, "that it's your day off, and you've already provided me with a lovely meal and a lovely bed." She looked to see if either of them took that any way but literally, but their expressions remained stony. "It would be my pleasure to cook breakfast. Y'all go sit, and I'll cook."

When they tried to object, she reached out and grabbed each by the chest hair, twisting just enough to get their attention.

Their eyes bugged out and their jaws dropped, but they consented to sit together at the table.

Lea chatted away, pulling eggs and sausages out of the fridge — remarkably clean for a pair of guys, but hey, firemen know about hygiene, right? She had the sausages frying and was whipping the eggs when the sun broke through the clouds that were the only evidence of the previous night's storm. "Man," she sighed, taking in the golden light that washed over the small woods behind the apartment, feeling the warmth on her gloriously weary body, "will you look at that. Just gorgeous."

She hadn't really said it for their benefit, and so she hadn't really expected them to answer, but still, she was surprised when all she heard from behind her was a quiet choking sound.

Both of them were staring at her, jaws dropped, eyes wide.

Oh. Fuck. Silk robe. She started to try to make her silhouette a bit more modest, but then thought, What the fuck, why not? Standing there, knowing that they could see the outline of her body very clearly, she repeated. "Gorgeous. Don't you think?"

"Yes, ma'am," they both answered, making Lea laugh.

As the sausage sizzled away in the pan and the eggs cooked, she thought, Look as much as you want, gentlemen. One of you owns all of this already. And then a thought occurred to her that made her blush and grin: And if I can figure out who it was, maybe I'll give all of it to the other one tonight!

When she brought the breakfast to the table, both men kept their eyes glued to their food.

More's the pity, sighed Lea, as they ate in silence.

When they were done, Lea started to clear, but Sean stopped her. "Naw, you cooked, we'll clean."

"You should get ready for your interview," said Andy, very seriously.

And so Lea left them to it, grabbing her garment bag and retreating back to the bathroom.

In the bathroom, she took stock. No more thinking about hunky firefighters, she scolded herself. Time to go get yourself a job.

When she came out, hair tamed (more or less), makeup sparingly applied, battle armor on, ready to take on the world, the two men were still in the kitchen, which was indeed now clean. They still didn't seem to have anything to say to each other. They were standing, arms crossed, leaning against the counter.

"You look lovely, Lea," said Sean, which made her middle go soft.

"Gorgeous," added Andy, making it go warm.

"Thanks, boys." She took a deep breath, trying to focus on the interview, and not on their muscular torsos. "Wish me luck."

"Good luck," they said in unison, and away she went.

The interview went far better than Lea had even hoped. She hit it off immediately with the business manager, a sardonic, middle-aged Canadian with the unlikely name of Sassy ("It's Sally actually, but they started calling me Saskatchewan, which they then shortened, and it's kind of stuck.") By late morning, they were swapping war stories, and Sassy dragged Lea out of her office to show her through the entire building, introducing Lea to staff as they went — an army of fundraisers, marketers, and box office staff, then backstage to meet technicians and the wardrobe department, and finally into a rehearsal — a set designer was showing the cast what the stage was going to look like, so it must have been a read-through. When the cast took an Equity break, Sassy buttonholed Bob, the artistic director of the theater, and asked him to join her and Lea for a late lunch at the barbecue joint across the street.

Trying not to think too much about the fact that she was now having lunch with the senior management of a theater that Lea would kill to work at, she gnawed away at her pork ribs.

"I think this is how we keep Sassy here," said Bob with a broad smile.

"It's true," said Sassy, smirking. "Every time I want to head back to the great white north, someone drops a take-out bag of ribs on my desk, and I know I can't leave."

"We have our ways," Bob chuckled.

As they bantered on, Lea felt the sauce from the rib she was chewing on dribbling onto her chin, and she couldn't help but remember teasing Sean and Andy with just that image the previous night, couldn't help but remember their stunned expressions. Couldn't help but remember what happened after the lights went out.

"Well, something's got you smiling," Sassy said.

"It's the barbecue," said Lea as she dabbed at her chin. "I can see why you can't leave it behind."

They all laughed.

They offered her the job before she'd even finished eating, and she accepted on the spot. The pay wasn't great, and she'd have to leave California and her best friend, but the opportunity was too good to pass up.

"Are you going to need help finding a place to stay?" asked Sassy, clearing their sauce-soaked baskets.

"I... think I may have one lined up." This brought an even broader grin to Lea's face than before.

She called back to the apartment. One of them — she thought it was Andy — picked up, and before he could say more than "Hello," she shouted, "I got the job! Dinner tonight's on me!"

"Well, congratulations!" said whichever of the men was on the phone.

And before he could say anything more, she hung up and did a dance, right there in the restaurant.

When she walked back up the stairs to the apartment a couple of hours later, she had in one hand an enormous bag full of barbecue chicken from the same joint she'd had lunch at, with orders of fried okra and corn bread. In the other hand, she swung a bottle of Maker's Mark, with which she knocked against the door.

Just like the day before, a muffled voice called out, "C'me in! It's unlocked."

"Can't!" she called back. "Hands full!"

"Hold on," said a slightly closer voice, and the door swung open, revealing Sean, who was still wearing nothing but low-slung pajama bottoms.

Andy was sitting at the kitchen table, identically dressed.

"Haven't you guys even gotten dressed all day?" Lea laughed and gave Sean a sound kiss on the lips.

He looked astonished, but Andy scowled.

"None of that!" burbled Lea, dancing into the kitchen and giving him an equally sound smooch. That seemed to cheer him up. "Tonight, we're celebrating!" She held up the barbecue and the bourbon.

They were happy to go along with this plan, and were soon all stuffed and pleasantly buzzed. Between the warmth, the Southern humidity, the food, and the alcohol, Lea was getting sweaty, but she couldn't have cared less. She was hoping to get a whole lot sweatier. Now which of you was my mystery man last night? she found herself wondering as she took off her jacket and tossed it in the general direction of the pullout. And am I going to get him to fuck me again, or am I going to try out the other one. Or...

She looked back at the two men, whiskey-wild thoughts bouncing through her head.

They were both staring at her. At her chest. Both licking their lips.

When she looked down, she saw that sweat had made her white silk blouse all but translucent. The lace bra showed clearly through. She grinned at them. "Well, gentlemen, like what you see?"

They both looked back up at her, hunger and shock plain on their faces.

Lea stood and walked around to their side of the table, unbuttoning her blouse as she went. "I have a confession to make, guys."

"Oh?" said Sean with a gulp, his eyes following her fingers' journey down from button to button.

Andy's eyes were still on Lea's tits.

"Uh-huh. I had a visitor in my bed last night."

Both men turned bright red and looked down at their feet.

Aha! Gotcha! "I got fucked good. And hard. And long."

They both gulped.

"Now, it was dark last night, and so I couldn't see just who this mystery lover was, and so all today, I've been trying to figure out." She knelt between them. "Was it you, Andy?" She touched him on the knee and tried not to laugh when he jumped. "Or you, Sean?" She ran her fingers up the inside of his thigh and he let out a choking sound.

"And as we were eating that wonderful barbecue tonight, I've remembered something. Do you want me to tell you what it was?" She slid her hand slowly up their thighs, so that all they could do was nod. "Well, I'm sure as firefighters you must have to study a lot about anatomy and such."

They nodded again.

She trailed her fingertips up onto their bellies. That stopped them. "Know what a G-spot is, boys?"

Again they both nodded.

"What good boys you are. Well, the G-spot is located at the front wall of a woman's puuuuusssssy." She drew the word out, trailing her fingers down the tops of their outside legs. "Now last night, I was sleeping on my belly when my lover woke me and, oooh, that was how he fucked me, and, oooooo, that long. Hard. Cock." Her fingers circled back up the insides of their legs. Sweat dripped from Sean's nose and Andy's cleft chin. "It stimmmm-ulated my G-spot — remember, on the front of my body, and — " She gave a low moan. "It felt soooo good. It made me come soooo hard!"

Her fingers reached their crotches; this time she pushed underneath, cupping their balls, which jumped in her hands, evoking gasps as they spread their legs to give her easier access. Such good boys.

"And then," she sighed, feeling her own crotch beginning to overflow at the bounty before her, "I got fucked again. On my back this time." One of them gasped. "And it was slow. And sweet. And aaaaaagonizingly good, and he did it again, his cock making that little spot in my pussy feel... Mmm... I came again, so hard I passed out."

She looked up at them as she juggled their testicles. Their eyes were closed, their jaws slack. "Now, gentlemen, do you know what I've realized?"

They shook their heads.

"Oh, now, gentlemen, I think you have. I think you have figured out what it took me alllllllll day to work out." She began to run her hands up the fronts of the pajamas. Oh, yes. I got it. I win! "Open your eyes please."

They both did, each gazing at her hand pressing against his crotch.

"Now, gentlemen, for this demonstration to work, you shouldn't be looking at your own equipment. Look at your roommate's."

Sean's gaze shifted smoothly to Andy's lap. Andy's locked pleadingly onto Lea's.

"Now, now, Andy, if you're a good boy, you know you'll get a reward, don't you?"

"Uh-huh," he gasped, sounding in fact very young. Very eager to please. And very horny. He pulled his eyes away from hers and looked down at where the tip of Sean's cock was pushing above the waistband of his pants.

"Here's what I realized, gentlemen." Now she stroked their growing erections, urging them on. "I realized that I came twice from having my G-spot stimulated." She slid each hand up to where each cock had now pushed past the waist of the pajama bottoms; she circled the tips with her fingers. "Once on my belly. And once on my back. And what does this tell us, gentlemen?"

"Both of us," sighed Sean, eyes half lidded but still locked on Andy's cock. "We both — aah!"

She had wrapped her hand around that long cock, which was now poking him in the belly button, and begun to stroke it.

He moaned and threw his head back, no longer able to watch.

As she continued to stroke him, she teased the uncircumcised head of Andy's, which was pushing away from his body as if desperate for more. "Do you see how good boys are rewarded, Andy?"

"Uh-huh." His eyes were still glued on the spectacle of Lea's hand milking Sean's long, freckled erection.

"Now," Lea pouted, "what I really want is one of these beautiful cocks in my mouth." She let loose a sigh. "But then I wouldn't be able to do as good a job with the other, and that wouldn't be any fun, would it?"

"Nuh-uh," they both grunted.

"I know! I'll suck the first one of you that helps me jerk the other off!"

Sean started to lift his hand, but — as Lea had guessed — Andy's shot out faster, grabbing Sean's erection at the base while she was at the head.

Andy's hand slid up to meet Lea's, and then, together, they traveled down again. Well, fuck, good thing you're so long, Sean! she thought as they began to stroke him.

Sean screamed, and Lea felt a splash of pre-cum spill over her knuckles.

"What a good boy you are, Andy! If you help me just a little more... Look, Sean! Look at both our hands on your beautiful, long cock."

Seemingly against his will, Sean's eyes pushed themselves back open. "Aww... Fuck."

In unison, Lea and Andy sped up; Andy seemed to be as proficient and energetic at jacking off as he was at fucking, because Sean soon started thrusting into their hands. His cockhead was slick; it was dark, dark red.

Sean stopped, held his breath, and then... "FUCK!" A rope of thick, white cum spewed over Lea's hand, landing in a long rivulet that started at one of Sean's nipples and ran down nearly to his navel.

Grinning up at him, Lea ran a finger through the cum and brought it to her lips. She licked it off. "Mmm."

"Lea," Andy whimpered.

"Don't worry, sweet boy. I'm going to give your reward now, don't you worry." Turning toward Andy, she worked to free his cock from the flannels that were holding it back; it was pushing out toward her like a dog pulling at its leash.

The PJs didn't want to let it go.

Finally, he pushed the offending pants down to his knees.

"Thanks, Andy," purred Lea, grasping his cock in both hands and bending forward to kiss the head.

"Damn," he gasped. "Good gawd damn."

Slowly, carefully — trying to think through how having a cock that curved down your throat was going to be different — she slowly sucked him in, and he continued to cuss a blue streak.

She discovered that actually, for such a big cock, Andy's was relatively easy to take into her mouth, because of the reverse curve. She was just beginning to give herself over fully to giving him a blow job that would repay the mind-blowing fuck that he'd treated her to the night before when a hand began to slide up the inside of her thigh — from the back.

"Aw, sweetheart," whispered Sean into her ear. "You have no idea how fucking hot you look, that pretty mouth stretched around his big ol' thang."

She moaned, mouth full of thang, incredibly nimble fingers exploring her crotch.

"What reward'll you give me, Lea," Sean whispered on, his other hand gliding just over her belly, her breasts, "if I help you suck this country boy off."

Releasing the dick in question from her mouth but not her hands, she groaned, "Anything you fucking want."

"Anything?"

"Yup." Not wanting to lose herself in those blue eyes, in the feeling of those strong, gentle fingers on her flesh, or the thought of that cock… She went back to sucking on Andy's equally lovely pound of flesh.

"What I want, Lea," said Sean, fingers scintillating as he leaned forward with her and gave one of Andy's heavy balls a slow lick. "What I've wanted since I met you seven years ago…" He sucked the testicle into his mouth and released it, causing Andy to howl and a dollop of bitter pre-cum to splash into Lea's mouth. "What I want, baby, is you." He ran his tongue up the length of Andy's erection until his mouth met hers; together they devoured Andy, whose fingers tangled in both heads of hair.

And as they kissed around Andy's cock — a kiss that Lea too had been dreaming about for seven years, though she'd never anticipated the swelling cock head pressing between and through their lips — Sean moved Lea's panties smoothly to the side, slipped his once-more hard cock smoothly into her, and for a moment — just one endless, timeless moment — the whole fucking world was absolutely fucking perfect.

Six months later, and it was football season, and so Lea knew where she'd find them — where she hoped she'd find them — after she'd finished house-managing the Sunday matinee: watching the game, sitting at the edge of the pullout they all now shared.

Well, Sean was sitting.

Andy was kneeling between Sean's thighs sucking at his roommate's long, gorgeous, spotted dick.

Fuck, thought Lea, how the fuck did I get so lucky? "So, Sean, you win a bet, or lose one?"

Her lover's eyes were half-closed from the pleasure that their other lover was giving him. "Won it. Idiot thought the Falcon's'd score on the last drive."

"Never bet against the San Francisco team, Andy, don't you know that?" laughed Lea, dropping her clothes to the floor and sliding up behind Andy, taking his semi-hard cock in hand, working to make sure that there was nothing semi about it. Once it was fully erect, she sidled her way between them.

Three for Three

Andy moaned, and Sean's cock popped free; Lea licked at it even as Andy moved behind her and pushed that wonderful inverted thang of his into her weeping cunt. "Holy fuck," she cried into Sean's cock head. Panting, she said, "Now, I hope you boys left some for me?"

They both gasped, "Yes, ma'am."

Swallowing Sean as Andy began to plow her from behind, she thought, What good boys you are!

And then thought became unimportant, because the whole fucking world was absolutely fucking perfect once more.

As it absolutely fucking always should fucking be.

K.D. West: I love firemen. Don't you? :-)
By the way, I've got more stories on this trio coming down the pike. We just released the next one, The Visitor Comes Home — there's a sneak peak at the back of this book.
To find out when the next is coming, keep an eye on my blog or on Stillpoint/Eros, or follow me on Facebook, Twitter (@KDWestWrites), Pinterest, Google+, or Tumblr.

Over the Top

A Friend (or Two) in Need Is a Friend (or Two) Indeed

The scratching sound from the ceiling begins again, and Danny groans. Within a minute, a soft, rhythmic thumping joins in time with the scraping, and he curls in upon himself, trying to bury his head under the pillow.

He could have chosen the cabin's upstairs bedroom — the one that is usually Danny's mom and dad's — but he thought it was polite to let Luz and Jamie have it. It is bigger, after all.

A soft sigh from above penetrates his pillow, and he finds himself answering it with a whimper.

They've been planning on coming up here after graduation, just the four of them, for a year. It's been a kind of schoolboy fantasy of being grownups, running off to the woods for a couple of weeks, away from the world, away from parents.... No one to watch who slept in which bedroom.

Finally. Fucking. Finally, finally fucking. Fantasy, sure, but unspoken promise as well. Sex in the cabin. Sex by the lake. Two couples, each doing what couples do.

Only that was before Suzie and Danny decided to be mature and break it off, since they were going to different colleges and long-distance relationships never work. Danny was the idiot to start that conversation. Suzie somberly told him two days before they left that she'd taken a job waiting tables with her friend Alice, the ditz, so she wouldn't be coming and making things uncomfortable. So: one couple. And Danny. No more schoolboy fantasy. Not for him, anyway.

Besides, even an idiot like Danny can see that Luz clearly isn't a schoolboy. Strictly speaking, neither are Jamie and Danny any more. And Jamie and Luz have been acting very much their age.

A giggle upstairs breaks the steady rhythm of scrape-sigh-thud, scrape-sigh-thud.

Blessedly, Danny has only actually walked in on them once, the second day after they came up to the woods. Danny was just coming back from a run around the lake, and his friends had apparently surprised themselves by succumbing to their own desires in the living room. The image of Luz's breasts gamboling against the cushion of the old couch that Jamie was leaning her over took an immediate and indelible place in Danny's imagination.

For two days after that, the three of them went about their business in utter silence. Cooking. Reading. Danny went fishing a lot. Not a word. Ms. Prince, the school librarian, would have been proud.

He's been very careful to let them know that he's going out for a walk every evening at sundown. That he won't be back for an hour or two. So they don't worry about him getting lost or anything.

And so since that one day, they've mostly restricted their more amorous activities to when he's out of the cabin. It hasn't stopped them from kissing and touching and sighing and making Danny want to hit them both.

And of course, every night, after they think he's asleep, Jamie and Luz engage in a particularly energetic, particularly bed-moving, particularly wall-banging fuck. Or two. Ten feet over his head.

In his mind's eye, Danny sees her now, right above him, on her hands and knees. Her bathrobe — was he too stupid to see her nipples through the fabric before, or is he just imagining them when he sees her now? — is piled up over her ass: round, and magnificent, jiggling with Jamie's thrusts, jiggling in time with her swaying breasts.

Jamie groans.

Maybe she is on her back, her thighs flushing dark on the insides where Jamie's hips slap against them, Jamie, his mouth open and eyes shut, Luz, her head thrown back...

Suzie, the soft, pale flesh of her belly beneath his lips, scent of flowers, a hungry whimper as he presses himself between her legs...

For the third time that day, Danny feels himself stiffening, his cock swelling within the hand that has unconsciously looped itself around the one piece of his flesh that no one else has ever poked at — flesh private to himself.

And, on thirteen miraculous occasions over the past year, Suzie. Her clever fingers slipping past the waistband of his jeans and evoking sensations that Danny would never have believed possible. All that sniggering about whacking off from the other guys, Jamie's sighing Luz's name in the bathroom, and Danny never knew. Never understood how flesh on flesh can perform such magic, can coax you out of yourself.

Now he knows. Now he can't stop. How can he have waited so long? And why can't he help himself now? What the hell is wrong with him?

The first time that Suzie rubbed him to explosion, after they'd been going out most of junior year, he cried after he came and she cradled him, kissing his forehead. And then he slipped his fingers beneath her skirt, past the elastic of her panties' leg to the moist, warm flesh beneath, and, trembling in the back seat of her parents' car, she showed him how to return the favor.

And he always stopped them from from going too quickly. From going too far.

Fuck.

That is where he longs to be now. Going too far. Cuddled against her secret flesh, his own cock pressing into her...

Luz screams Jamie's name, and the bed above slams against the wall one last time and skids to a stop.

Danny's fingers are stroking, grasping tightly at his cock — the head is dark red and the flesh stings with use and need. He looks down and growls in disgust at himself. I have to take a shower, he thinks, and with great, unwilling determination detaches hand from rod. A girl's high voice sighs Oh, oh, oh, and he can't tell if he's hearing Luz from the room above or Suzie in his own mind, and he knows that if he doesn't do something right now he will go crazy. Crazier. Over the top. And that whacking off isn't doing something. Not any more.

He stumbles into the bathroom and sheds his glasses and pajamas, jumping beneath the shower before he has time to think about the fact that it's going to be frigid; it's been a chilly summer up here in the mountains. The cold water sears his flesh and deflates his erection, and the pain of its shrinking is almost a relief.

Danny's parents talk about love way too much. Their doormat read All You Need Is Love. Love is happiness and Love is the greatest power in the universe on the fridge. Blah, blah, blah. Love.

Danny spent so many of his school year alone. Embraced the fact that no one gave a shit about him except to make fun of the nerd in the Harry Potter glasses. Love wasn't something he wanted to think about. But now... Now he can feel love — his love for Suzie, even though he broke it off with her. Hell, his love for Jamie and Luz — he can feel all of that love twisting him, warping him like the wet clay that Mr. Benson showed them how to shape on a wheel.

Clay: the cool, smooth feel of the wet earth beneath his fingers felt good, and shapes formed — magically formed — as the clay spun between his hands: a lovely flower-blossom cup.

That blew up in the kiln. But Danny didn't care. Much. He made something. And the feel of it, alive and slippery...

Suzie's slit, slick and soft and warm beneath his fingers. Her fingers, slim and strong around his shaft...

Luz's breasts, shock waves rippling through them as Jamie thrusts into her, their love and lust animal and terrible, their faces twisted...

"FUCK!" With a frustrated scream, Danny turns off the water and collapses in the fiberglass tub with a bang. His cock is as erect and demanding now as it ever was, and Danny knows it won't go away, but knows too that if he tries to take care of it now while it is wet or uses soap it will only shred his overused skin until he bleeds and that still won't satisfy its hunger. His hunger. His desire. He kicks the wall of the bath, and then kicks it again. And again. "SHIT!"

The door bursts open and a wide-eyed, wild-haired Luz flies in, Jamie just behind her. Her gown is at best haphazardly closed and even as Danny scrambles to hide himself, to cover his adamant shame, he cannot help but notice a berry-colored blur of a nipple bouncing near the hem.

"Danny!" Luz gasps.

"You... You okay, bro?" asks Jamie, and the only mercy is that there isn't even the hint of a smirk in his friend's voice. "Sounded like you fell!"

"I'm f-f-fine," Danny manages to splutter, but he knows he isn't fooling them, lying there with tears flowing down his wet cheeks and his hands cupped over his engorged penis.

"Oh, Danny," Luz sighs, and her compassion only makes Danny feel worse — or perhaps she is merely giving him permission — and the floodgates open and Danny begins to weep in earnest.

Two sets of hands pull him up, lead him out of the tub, wrap him in a towel and dry him off. Two sets of arms pull him into a warm, trembling hug.

Love.

Through the towel, Danny's cock strains against Luz's round, wide belly.

"Danny," Jamie says, and Danny can hear the hesitancy in his friend's voice. "Danny, how can we...?"

"We're so sorry, Danny. We didn't think of... Of how loud we were being. Right above you. That really wasn't fair of us."

"No, no, no, it's not you," Danny hisses. "It's me. I'm just... twisted. I'm sick. I..."

"You miss her, don't you, Danny," says Jamie, and Danny feels what little blood isn't pooled in his pelvis rushing to his face.

They know. They know how he's aching for Suzie. How he's regretting...

Rubbing himself bloody thinking about...

"Danny, we understand." It is Luz's voice this time and new shame floods Danny, knowing that Luz knows. That Luz, who thinks of him as a friend, as a good guy, knowing that she knows that he dreams of girls' pussies and asses and breasts. Of Luz's pussy even when he dreams of Suzie. "We're sorry, Danny."

"Maybe..." Jamie mutters. "Maybe we can help you out a bit. Maybe Luz..."

"Jamie?" snaps Luz, and Danny feels his innards tear.

"I know what it's like," Jamie snaps back with deadly urgency.

"Being around you for months. Wanting to touch you, to... to fuck you and not being able to and feeling like I was going to bloody explode. Like if someone didn't touch me, I was going to fucking die. For real, die."

Danny moans, and he feels Luz shift against him and hates himself for noticing that her cotton-covered nipples are stiffening against his chest and shoulder. Hates himself for noticing that the two of them reek of sex.

"Jamie, are you suggesting...?" Luz begins, but a wet sound closes her mouth; Jamie has kissed his talk-first girlfriend into silence. The nipples press harder against Danny's flesh, and it is only because he is terrified and because the two of them are already holding him that he restrains his hands from grasping those breasts, from feasting on those nipples, from pulling her... "Danny," Luz says quite breathily. "Danny, I... I could... um, help you. If you wanted. If that didn't seem too disgusting."

"Disgusting?" Danny finally manages to say, an angry laugh. "Why the fucking hell would the idea of you touching me be disgusting?"

"Well," Luz murmurs, "I know I'm not exactly as pretty as Suzie..."

Jamie begins to grumble but Danny once again beats him to it. "Hell of a fucking lot you know. You're fucking gorgeous, Luz. Jamie's the luckiest fucking bastard in the world, and he knows it." Danny can feel her shiver against him, and it doesn't help matters. "But... You two love each other. And I... I love Suzie, and I fucking sent her away like a fucking idiot and I fucking miss her so fucking much and I'm so fucking horny I can't take it, and you two, I don't want you not to enjoy... But the sound or even the thought of the sound fills my fucking head and my fucking body and it makes me so bloody hard, and I... FUCK!" Danny collapses in frustration against his friends' embrace, furious with his body that it doesn't seem to care that Luz is Jamie's girlfriend, not his, that Suzie is the one he wants. Furious with his body that what it really wants to do just now is push his friend up against the counter and shove itself into whatever hole is available.

"Danny," Luz says, and it is the rational, logical Luz voice, the AP Calc voice, and Danny thanks whatever stars are watching over him, because that voice returns him to something like himself. "I'd be happy to help you — but only if you think that it would help. That it wouldn't just make you feel worse."

Too desperate to be shocked, Danny moans, "Please."

Jamie grunts and Luz gives a quick gasp. "Really?"

"Please."

"All right, Danny. All right. I'd be... Um. Wow." Leaning forward, she gives him a quick, fluttery kiss on the lips, and he can feel her grinning against his mouth. Then, stepping back out of the group embrace, she squares her shoulders. "Jamie, Danny, I'll only do this if I know you both understand that it doesn't change anything. That we're still... friends."

"Yeah," said Jamie, and his voice is low with something Danny would guess in a different situation was anger.

Not wanting to think too hard about it, Danny nods emphatically.

Luz speaks again, and her voice is edging higher; she clearly knows they are talking about doing something terribly dangerous. Something potentially really stupid. "Good. And I won't... won't fuck you, Danny, because I know Suzie would never forgive me, and I wouldn't forgive myself. And I won't do anything unless Jamie stays. I don't want you imagining things that didn't happen, love. And I don't want you feeling like we're doing anything sneaky, Danny. Because I..." Something chokes her voice off, and Danny wishes that he could see the blob that is her face more clearly. "Do you both understand?"

In his peripheral vision, Danny sees Jamie's fuzzy profile nodding vigorously. He follows suit.

Trembling hands — Luz's, smooth and fine — take his shoulders and move him back. "Maybe... Here, Danny, why don't you have a seat?"

Suddenly, he is feeling cold — colder than he did in the shower. Shaking, he complies. The wooden lid of the toilet presses up flat against his balls, pushes his erection up into the towel.

Luz is moving in front of him, arranging the bathmat, kneeling down.

"Wait... Uh..." Danny says with a swallow. "Could I...? I'd like to, um, see. May I have my glasses?" Out of the indistinct fog, Danny sees a large hand clutching the familiar black frames. Jamie's hand. "Thanks, bro."

"'Snothing, bro."

Sliding on his glasses, Danny sees them both: Luz, her dark skin pale, eyes wide and bright; Jamie dark with some emotion that Danny can't even begin to fathom. "Guys... You don't have to do this, Luz. I don't... Jamie, it's okay. I'll survive."

A grin flashes across his friend's wide face and he says, "I... I don't mind at all, Dan. As long as it's okay with Luz." He strokes her hair, and she gives a small smile. "It's actually kind of... a turn-on, you know?"

Now Luz's face darkens.

Danny doesn't know, but he doesn't want to ask, doesn't think he can take talking about this much longer.

"Do you know what fellatio is, Danny?" When he shakes his head, Luz continues tentatively. "A, um, blow job?"

"Oh. Uh. Yeah."

She runs her fingers along his towel-covered leg. "Would you like me to do that for you?"

Choking on his heart, Danny glances up at Jamie.

Jamie is grinning even more broadly. "Trust me, Danny, you would like it. Her mouth is amazing."

Gulping for air, Danny gasps, "Okay."

Luz's brown eyes search up into his, and Danny is struck for the first time at just how different this brown is from the bright cinnamon in Suzie's irises. Luz's eyes are dark, piercing... and uncertain, just now.

"Luz," Danny pleads.

She favors him with a nearly imperceptible grin and peels back the towel.

There's a sharp intake of breath, and Danny has no idea which of the three of them took it.

Her fingers, ink-stained, brown, and long, reach out and touch his cock gently.

Another gasp, and this time Danny knows it's his.

"Does mine look that fucking huge?" Jamie groans, his face dark again.

"I'm not going to play adolescent male comparison games, Jamie. But yes, yours is quite nice."

Her fingers curl around the cock they're both staring at and suddenly Danny can't look anymore. "Oh, god, Luz!"

It's easy to forget, rubbing your prick night after night, day after day, hour after hour, that having someone else rub it is a very different, very nice feeling.

And then Luz — prim, perfect, polite Luz — lowers her mouth to the head of his cock. Circles the head with her tongue. Her eyes on his the entire time.

This is not a nice feeling. It is a feeling that is so good that it hurts.

"Oh, god," Jamie groans.

Suzie offered to do this once, at the end of yet another long make-out session (this one in the back seat of his parents' car), but Danny was so nervous and so eager that he'd spurted before she'd even gotten his fly all of the way down. Suzie didn't mind. At least she said she didn't.

Her lips over her teeth, Luz slowly takes Danny's head into her mouth; he can feel the flare of his helmet pressing against the roof of her mouth. Can feel the bursts of excited breath from her nostrils along his length.

Suzie's mouth, small and hot, her tongue against his, sharp-tipped and searching...

DNA has four base nucleotides. RNA does as well, but the complimentary base to adenine is uracil instead of...

"Oh, GOD!" Danny finds his hands fisting in Luz's bushy hair and it is only through a supreme effort of will that he keeps himself from pulling his friend's mouth all the way down the length of his cock. "Fuck, Luz!"

She pulls back off of him just a touch and beams when he whimpers. "Do you like that, Danny?"

"Oh, god! Fuck yesss!"

She takes him back into her mouth, deeper this time, and slowly begins to bob, her fist running up and down his shaft as her tongue swirls over his tip. Glorious.

One night, late, studying at Suzie's for the English final, Mr. Logan's which was notoriously impossible, and after Alice, Luz, and Jamie took off, and Suzie's little sister finally disappeared upstairs, Suzie pounced on him, straddling him in the couch, her hair blinding him, her crotch, thin cotton clad, grinding against his own until she shrieked and he screamed...

"Fuck, Luz, that's so fucking hot," Jamie cries out, and he moves up behind her, his hands running under the gown, a breast bouncing free. A hand running down past her belly, past where Danny can see.

Luz groans around Danny's cock.

"Suck his cock, babe," Jamie growls into her ear. "Take Danny's hard cock in that dirty, smart-ass, bookworm mouth and make him come."

Her eyes still locked on his, Luz's cheeks glow bronze as they fill and hollow. Shame? Desire? With the hand that had been resting on Danny's thigh, she reaches up and roughly squeezes his nipple.

A tingling, like the most painful pins-and-needles ever, a contraction deep within. Suzie, her eyes closed, her cheeks flushed bright red, nipples hard as diamonds as they pound their pelvises together, I'm yours, I'm yours!

"Suzie!"

Even after two rounds of masturbation earlier in the day, the force of the orgasm threatens to destroy Danny. His hips buck and a flood of warmth explodes out of him and into Luz's hot, soft mouth. Not just one pulse but a dozen, each releasing its own bit of the shadow that has been smothering him.

A brief cough, and Luz swallows, releasing his penis from that incredible mouth, staring up into Danny's eyes with a look of ferocious pride.

Then Jamie turns her to him and they kiss, and Danny can see her jaw working as she presses her tongue into Jamie's mouth. Danny's jism into Jamie's mouth.

And Danny can see their bodies arching together, kneeling there on the bathroom floor, the head of Jamie's cock poking purply out from the waistband of his pyjama bottoms. Luz's nipples appropriately enough the shape and size of pencil erasers against Jamie's chest. Her hands tangled in his mane of hair.

Danny stands on shaky legs. "Thanks, guys," he says, covering himself with the towel again. They break apart. Barely.

"Thank you, Danny," says Luz, blinking up at him, her voice low as he has never heard it.

"Hope it helped," Jamie grunts, biting the inside of his cheeks, and Danny smiles, knowing that they are both doing everything they can not to fuck at his feet.

"It did," he says with a smile, and leaves, closing the door behind him.

Once Danny returns to his bed — cursing the fact that he's forgotten his pajamas — he realizes that it has helped. But it hasn't.

The randy insanity into which Danny was about to lose himself is gone — the edge of it taken off, at least — but as he settles naked between the sheets he finds himself hard as ever. Thinking about Suzie. And about what's just happened.

Has he betrayed Suzie? Or Jamie?

How would he feel if he saw Suzie sucking off a friend of theirs — Jamie? Bill? What did she do with Bill? She never wanted to discuss it, and Bill was always unwilling to talk specifics about what he got up to with Suzie — out of fear of pissing Danny off as much as out of delicacy, probably, since everyone knew how Danny felt about her, even before he did. Did she take Bill in her mouth? She jerked Danny off expertly enough — had she practiced on their friend? Or on Luke Harris, the jerk she'd dated briefly sophomore year? Had either of them buried his fingers or tongue or cock in her sweet folds? She told Danny she was still a virgin, but what did that mean?

And what about now? They've texted and — very carefully and infrequently — written since graduation, but Danny had pulled the Spiderman, Harry Potter routine, making made it very clear that, feel for her as he still did, they couldn't be together just now. She said she wouldn't give up on him. But he has no claim on her. And he's been away out of cell range and without internet for nearly two weeks.

Maybe she's seeing someone. Maybe she is fucking him right now.

Would watching that excite Danny as watching Luz clearly excited Jamie?

No.

No, he'd want to kill the guy, and then himself.

Not Suzie. No. He couldn't blame her; he gave her free rein.

He loves her. Fuck. He loves her.

But he'd rather die than watch some other boy's dick press through her lips, or her... lips.

And yet he's just come in Luz's mouth. Not Suzie's. How is that fair?

And here he is, hard as iron again, and Danny knows that he can't go back to Luz, that she and Jamie are busy — they must have gone back up to the bedroom; he can hear the bed above him beginning to move again — and that he has no right with anyone but Suzie (small breasts bouncing on either side of my face), but he has no right with her...

Her thin lips tracing the length of his cock as his tongue traces the line of her cunt lips...

Clear liquid is spilling from the tip of his cock and — in spite of himself — Danny uses his palm to spread the slick stuff along his penis and he feels a kind of panic sweeping over him. What the fuck's wrong with you, Danny? Can't you leave it alone?

Apparently not.

Circling the nub of flesh at the front of her, her clit, flicking it, making her squirm, feeling her swallow him to the root...

Suzie.

Danny's cock swells, pulsing in his hand; not soon, this round. He'll last for a long, long time, and hate himself from beginning to end.

The beast within him stretches, pleased at being given so much exercise, its wings spreading at the thought of those thin, pale lips against his, of her tongue — salty with his come — dancing with his own, and he begins to wail, knowing that he can rub himself bloody, can rub the fucking thing right off, but that still wouldn't satisfy his need, his hunger. "Oh, god, Suzie!"

"Danny?"

Danny's eyes fly open. There she is, in the doorway, face barely visible through her wild, red hair, shirt open, eyes wide and face flushed. "Danny? Are you all right?" she pants, staring at his cock as she walks the three feet to the bed. "What the fuck...?"

He leans up and his lips find her lips. His hands find her breasts — heaving, nipples diamond-hard.

"Here?" he groans into her mouth as he pulls the buttons off of the front of her shirt. He tastes her, breathes her in, stunned to find that all of his senses agree: Suzie is here. Still, he has to make sure. "Not hallucinating, you're really here?"

"Yup." She chuckles into his mouth and throws one leg across his bare waist. "Miss me, Danny?"

"Oh, fuck, Suzie, so much."

He can feel her lips smiling against his. Her hands find his bare ass and pull him to her until the head of his cock begins to press into the slick cleft that it has been straining to plow for months. She's not wearing panties.

"Wait. Wait. Suzie. Hold on," he mumbles into her mouth.

"Don't want to hold on. Want to fuck you."

"Suzie. Shit. Want you so much..."

"Want you too. Missed you. Want you so fucking much..." She mashes her slit along the shaft of his cock. "Don't want to fuck this? I'm on the Pill, have been for... Or... Want to stick that beautiful thing of yours in my backside, Danny? You can. I'm yours. My ass. My cunt. My mouth. My tits. Anything you want. All yours. But please, Danny," she urges, an edge of crazy desperation in her voice. "Fuck first, talk later. Or fuck and talk. But please...!"

He may be an idiot, but Danny di Angelo is not completely stupid. He spears up into her tight heat. "Fuck!" they both shout, and then, after a moment of stunned, still silence, they laugh and move, their pelvises finding a comfortable rhythm almost immediately. Danny feels her laughter around his cock, and that makes him happier than anything, happier even than the smooth, soft flesh that is clutching his penis.

They roll, and he can feel how deeply he's pushed into her tight, hot...

As much as being inside of Luz's mouth transcended his own ministrations, this outdoes that: body against body, her cunt tight and grasping around his thrusting cock, her breasts bouncing against his chest, mouth searching mouth and it's Suzie....

Luz. Fuck. He's gone from one girl to another before his dick has even had time to dry.

Pelvis still rocking against pelvis, he pushes back just enough to look down on her. Sees her, beautiful beyond words, eyes and mouth wide with wonder. "I love you so much, Suzie. I never said. I'm sorry." As if to give her the measure of his love, he withdraws his cock to the tip, almost to the point of losing contact, and then plunges it back in to her. Sheathing himself in her. Losing himself in her. And every ripple of her as he does is like some ridiculous, miraculous explosion; he feels like a never-ending Roman candle, flares and sparks of sensation connecting him to Suzie.

"Love you, too, Danny. It's okay." Her eyes fly wide as he thrusts back in again. "Fuck!"

They laugh again, but Danny feels a tinge of sadness coloring his joy. "Didn't hurt you, did I? Aren't girls...?" A thought passes through his head and he mentally tries to bat it away, banish it.

Her eyes glitter mischievously. "Not girls who've been riding for ten years, silly boy."

"Riding? Who've you been riding?" It's a joke. A tease. But it isn't, and he regrets it as soon as it leaves his mouth.

Her hands push back on his hips, stopping his thrusts. "Hey! They're a hell of a lot bigger than you, and they walk on four feet." Suzie's bright brown eyes narrow and darken. "For that matter, boys are supposed to explode within the first thirty seconds, not bang away for ten minutes. Anyone been riding you while I've been serving pizza, pining away for you at home, di Angelo?"

"No!" Danny says, but his face falls, and she sees it and her chin juts out dangerously.

"What's going on, Danny?" she asks, twisting away from him so that they almost disengage.

"No, Suzie, stop. Please. Talk while fucking, right?" He kisses her and holds her tight. After a moment he feels her legs pull him back in.

"Okay," she sighs, her face still not quite open. "So what gives, Danny? What's turned you into Mr. Everlast?"

Sighing, Danny looks into her eyes, willing her to believe the truth. "I've been dying here, Suzie, thinking of you every day. Every night."

She peers at him, gauging his honesty. Slowly, she begins to rock against him again, and he groans. "Thinking about me, were you, Danny?"

"More than thinking, Suzie."

She grins, a hint of wariness flashing in her eyes. "Always said you were a jerk-off."

Now it is his turn to laugh. "Yeah, well, I pretty well earned that title lately."

She leans up and kisses his nipple. "Poor boy."

"But... Suzie..."

She looks at him, more trusting but nervous. Their movement together is small, now, but exquisite. The sparks all the brighter for being fewer.

"Tonight..."

"Tonight, what? You pick up some local girl to fill your lonely nights, Danny? Fucking some mermaid out on the lake? Sasquatch?"

"No, Suzie, no, it's not like that, I swear, I..."

A shudder passes through her. "Just tell me, Danny. You fucked some girl —"

"What? No." They are belly to belly, resting, neither moving. This really isn't how Danny wanted his first time with Suzie — with anyone — to go.

"Two weeks, I've been sitting at home, or at the fucking pizzeria, missing you, nobody to talk to except Alice." Suzie's best friend aside from Danny and Luz, and very sweet, but probably the most boring girl on the face of the earth. "And I was lying in bed tonight and I thought, fuck it. Fuck it. Stole Mom's car, drove two hours with one hand on the wheel and the other in my crotch, and boom, here I was, ready for ravishing."

"You were in your bed?" Danny grins, beginning to slide into her again.

Her eyes get bright and cagey. "Didn't say it was my bed, now did I?"

The beast is back in Danny's chest, scaly and furious, as he thinks about her state when she arrived. Clothes undone. Face flushed. Cunt wet and ready. Nipples hard as pebbles. "No? Whose, then, Suzie?" Even after a two hour drive...

He is beginning to thrust harder, and she meets his thrusts, her hips slamming against his. "Jealous, Danny?"

Furious as he is, he is also ashamed. And feeling very, very good everywhere except inside of his head. And he owes her the truth, whatever she has been doing; he was the one who broke it off with her. As he is about to tell her about Luz, about Jamie's offer and Luz's mouth, there is a loud yelp from above the ceiling and a crash that shakes dust from the beams.

She blinks. "What the fucking hell was that?"

He can't help but grin. "Jamie. Luz. I think they just broke the bed."

She favors him with a red-cheeked smirk. "You're fucking joking."

Shaking his head, Danny laughs. "No, honest. They've been going at it so hard lately, I'm amazed it's lasted this long."

"So they finally managed it! Wasn't sure Luz'd have the balls. Way to go...!"

He withdraws, and then plunges in deep once more.

"Can't blame them," Suzie says, shuddering again. "This feels pretty damned good."

"Yeah." Danny suddenly remembers the whip-like, rolling motion that Jamie had been employing in the living room. *I wonder...*

As his pubic bone bucks against her clit, Suzie's eyes open wide and she gasps. "OH! Fuck, Danny... Just... I don't care who you fucked, I really don't, but please don't ever do this with anyone else, okay?"

"Don't want to..." Amazingly, Danny can feel pressure building up behind his balls, the balls that are slapping against Suzie's ass. *Time to confess and demand confession later. This is where he wants to be.* "No one else. Ever. Never fucked anyone."

She is clawing at his back, the high, bubbling sigh in his ear signaling that she is as close as he is. "Me either, Danny. I swear. You're. Only. Boy. 'Ve ever. Fucked."

"Good!" he cries. And he is crying, his cock plunging into her, his heart opening out to her. "Couldn't stand it, Suzie. Kill me. If you..."

"Ah!" The bed is rocking against the wall, and Danny knows precisely how it would sound if he were on the floor below. If there were a floor below.

"Yours!" they both howl and orgasm overcomes them both and they collapse, tangled in each other irredeemably.

Some time later, Danny becomes aware again of time.

"I love you, Danny." Her voice sounds low and moist.

Danny's glasses seem to have flown off of his face. Sweat, tears and astigmatism make her a pink-and-orange blur. He leans to the center, knowing he'll find something to kiss. Her nose. "Love you, Suzie."

They lie there, each gasping for breath. Finally — finally — Danny's cock begins to soften, satisfied at last. He starts to withdraw, but she holds him close, arms and legs clasping.

"So," she says, her voice small, "who do I have to thank for getting you all... ready for me?"

He hides his face behind her ear. "Luz," he whispers.

"Luz!" she gasps. "Danny, how could you two do that to Jaime?"

"It was his idea."

"What?"

As he tells her — as he describes the whole evening, including the two early solo sessions, the cold shower, and their friends' solution — Suzie's grip on him begins both to tighten and to soften, and he realizes that she's now crying, she, who never cries. "Oh, Danny, you poor son of a bitch. I'm so sorry."

"Don't be," he murmurs, tasting the salt of her tears as he kisses her. "My fault. And... You're here now."

"I'm not going away, Danny. I won't leave you again. I won't."

Danny rests his forehead against hers. Can feel her heart beating against his chest. Around his cock. Being apart from her nearly drove him over the cliff. Can he stand to do that again? On the other hand, they're going to colleges three time zones apart. And everyone says long-distance relationships don't work. And high-school romances don't last. And... On the other hand... "Let's think about it. We'll talk about it tomorrow. I just... I know I can't think straight just now."

"Oh!" Suzie says and chuckles. "I have that effect on you, do I?"

"Yes. Your body is kind of amazing. And... You. You make it so that nothing else in the world is real. "

"Oh. I... Thank you, Danny."

"Thank me?"

She is crying again.

"It's okay, Suzie. Really. Come on. I love you."

The sound that escapes Suzie's mouth is a high, keening sigh, not unlike the sound she makes when she's about to come; but this time she sounds as if her heart is breaking, and he pulls her tight against him. He rolls on his back, her body still joined to his, her face still buried in his neck. For a long time, he rocks her there, kissing her, stroking her back.

Eventually, she stills, only hiccoughing occasionally. She leans back and sits up on him, his cock still planted limp inside of her.

Her hair blazes against the dull white of the plaster ceiling, but her skin is so pale that he can barely tell where she begins and ends. Her eyes, though — those he can see, black smudges. And her mouth and nipples, bright in a sea of white and softer pink. "It's so amazing to see you without your glasses," she sighs. "Your eyes are so beautiful. So bottomless. You really can't see without them?"

He shakes his head.

"Oh. Well, it's probably just as well. Because... Danny, you've explained the state you were in tonight..."

A heavy weight suddenly settles into Danny's middle — and it's nothing to do with the light pressure of Suzie's pelvis against his. "Suzie, I told you. I don't blame you. I broke things off with you. You had every right to see any boy in town. I just — "

Her hands clutch at his shoulders. "Danny! Believe me, please! I haven't been seeing — or kissing, or boffing, or blowing, or touching — any fucking boys. I swear — "

"Thank god," Danny moans, reaching up to her face. "I'm not like Jamie, Suzie. The idea of another boy's hands on you... When Jamie and I saw you and Bill kissing at the junior prom, I wanted..." He takes a shaky breath. "I felt as if I had a fucking dragon inside of me trying to claw its way out and kill him. And that was before you and I ever... The idea of you with any other boy is more than I can stand, Suzie. I'm sorry. It's stupid."

"It's not stupid, Danny," Suzie says, touching his cheek. "It's the sweetest thing I've ever heard. But..."

"What, Suzie?" Dread settles into Danny's gut again. "Please just tell me so I don't have pictures of you and every boy in town in my head. Just tell me who."

"Please, Danny. Promise you won't be... Promise, no matter how upset you are, you'll forgive me."

He takes a deep breath. "I promise."

"What if..." She takes a slow, steadying breath. "Danny, what if it wasn't a boy?"

The monster is back inside of him, but it isn't cold or scaly; it's hot and chuckling. "What?" A grown man? No, Danny knows that's not what she means...

"Alice. Alice's the only friend that I could talk to about you, Danny, she's the only one I could really talk to, and she's your friend too, and she's been very... I was with her, tonight, and she was the one who said I should come... Um... She's been so... helpful."

Helpful. Like Luz.

Danny's cock twitches inside of Suzie and begins to grow.

"Oh!" she gasps.

Alice's wide mouth on Suzie's breasts. Her fingers circling Suzie's clit as Suzie calls out Danny's name. "Oh, god, Suzie..."

"Danny?" Suzie laughs, relieved. She begins to move up and down on his incredibly-erect-once-again penis, her skirt splashing against Danny's belly. "Fuck, Danny. Guess you didn't mind too much." Alice's tongue running along Suzie's open, wet lips. Pressing her fingers gently into Suzie while Suzie pinches at her nipples... just as she is doing now. Alice's white ass high in the air...

He begins to thrust up into her — fluid from their first fuck flowing down — and Suzie moves against him. "Feels so... Fuck! You're an over-the-top, twisted fucker after all, aren't you, Danny-boy?"

"You have no idea," grunts Danny. "I have no idea. But let's find out."

The Trouble with Triplets, pt. I

A Cautionary Tale —

A sneak peek at the beginning of a new threesome story!

K.D. West: This is part of one of my Erotic Tales/ Love Letters *stories. In these stories, Ken is writing his young lover (and former student) Allison while she's away at college, sharing the stories of his adventures as a young man.* When he writes this letter, she has been teasing him with the idea of a threesome between Allison, Ken, and Allison's BFF and sometime innamorata Jordan. Here's the beginning of Ken's response; it doesn't go in quite the direction that Ken expected, but I think he found the ending... satisfying.*

I've participated — or almost participated — in three threesomes, only one of which was actually my idea.

Not one of them turned out the way any of us expected.

The first two were both ideas of Cindy's, which shouldn't have been a surprise, though it was at the time.

The summer that I first met her, we were playing Viola and Sebastian in a local production of Twelfth Night.

That summer was the first time that I fell in love. Oh, I loved Dana. I still do. But with Cindy it was if the color leached out of everything else in the room when she walked in.

The problem was, I wasn't the only one in the cast following her around like a duckling. One of the other guys in the cast, Michael, who was playing Antonio, rarely left her elbow. He and I got along well, we hung out together during the show and after.

About a week after the show opened, we were at a local bar — I was underage, but no one ever asked. As had become our habit, Cindy, Michael and I had split off from the rest of the cast, and were hanging at a table at the back of the bar, trading stories about nothing in particular. "I have to tinkle," said Cindy, standing. "Don't talk about me took much."

Once she had gone, Michael turned to me and said, "You okay with me going after Cindy?"

I swigged my beer, thought about it for a moment. "Not sure. You okay if I went after her?"

A rueful smile on his face, Michael shook his head and raised his bottle. "Best man wins?"

I clicked my beer to his. "Best man wins."

When Cindy sauntered back from the bathroom, I was still trying to come up with a first move in the chess game, but Michael beat me to it. "Hey, Cindy, a friend of mine over at River Shakes — " A Shakespeare festival just over the mountain from ours. " — just offered me a couple of comps to tomorrow's show of their Twelfth Night. Want to come?"

I gawked at him, at his audacity at getting off the mark so quickly. He shot me a wink.

Cindy sounded thrilled. "That'd be great! Jen, who's playing their Viola, is an old friend of mine." The first woman Cindy had ever fallen in love with — but I wouldn't find out about that until much later. Cindy reached out and grabbed my wrist. "You want to come too, Ken?" Turning back to Michael, she smiled. "I don't suppose your friend could manage another comp?"

Michael flashed me a look of what I hoped was mock annoyance and raised his bottle. "No problem."

I laughed and tapped his bottle once more with mine. Quoting from one of our scenes together, I said, "I can no other answer give than thanks!"

Michael grunted, but smiled back, and Cindy laughed her low, throaty laugh.

I was driving my dad's beat up old Triumph that summer, and so we all jumped in and rode over the treacherous road to River Shakes the next night and enjoyed the hell out of watching other peoples' takes on the roles that we were performing. While Cindy told her friend Jen very breathily how wonderful her performance had been, Michael and I chatted with our counterparts — Michael's part in their show had been played by a woman: Antonia. We laughed about the evident sexual tension between Antonio/a and Sebastian. Michael told them that our nickname for the character had been the Swishbuckler.

Michael and his counterpart were actually getting along well — really well. She was flirting with him like all hell. (The other Sebastian flirted with me for about thirty seconds before smiling at me, giving me a wink, and turning off the full-press charm. I've always had that affect on gay men.)

When Antonia started putting her hand on my friend's shoulder, I decided to see if I could press my advantage — and do him a favor at the same time. "Michael, Cindy and I have rehearsal for Cyrano tomorrow morning, we should get back."

As I'd hoped and expected, the Antonia said, "Oh, if you don't have rehearsal, Michael, I'm sure we could find someplace for you to spend the night." Her tone made it very clear that the someplace would be very warm and cozy.

Michael's jaw worked, and he looked over at me as if to say, Damn! How'd you manage that? "Uh, thanks, but I should get back too." He squeezed the woman's hand. "Maybe later in the run?"

She grinned. "Maybe."

"Hey, Cindy," Michael said, "you ready to head back? You and this prick have rehearsal tomorrow morning."

Cindy pouted, gave her friend a kiss on the cheek, and then pulled the two of us out toward where I'd parked the Triumph.

"Bye!" called the Antonia. The other Sebastian and I both laughed.

On the ride back, Cindy sat in the back and talked about the production we'd seen, both its strengths (Jen's Viola, in her mind) and its weaknesses (everything else).

Grinning, I looked over at Michael and said, "Actually, I thought the Antonia was great."

"Yes," granted Cindy, almost grudgingly. "She was pretty good."

"And she thought our Antonio was damned cute."

I thought for a moment that Michael was going to punch me. Good thing that I was at the wheel on a windy road.

"Well," said Cindy, throwing an arm around Michael's neck, "he is!"

Michael smiled smugly at me.

Then Cindy kissed me on the cheek. "And our Sebastian is much hunkier than theirs."

I smirked back at Michael.

We chatted and flirted through the rest of the drive.

We reached Cindy's place first — a house that the theater had found for her to house-sit. "It's not even midnight," she said. "Come on up and take a hot tub with me."

Michael and I looked at each other, both a little shocked by the invitation, and each unwilling to back down. "Sure," we both said.

While we waited for the tub to heat up, we drank beers and chatted. Well, Michael and I were both feeling a bit uncertain, so mostly Cindy talked. But she was very comfortable with that.

After a half hour, steam was rising off of the bubbling water. "Why don't you boys jump in," Cindy said as coquettishly as her husky contralto could manage. "I'll be right out."

Once she'd left the deck, Michael stripped down to his boxers. When I jumped into the hot tub commando, however, he pulled off the shorts with a look of grim determination.

We were so aware of each other that neither of us noticed Cindy stepping into the tub behind us. "Hi, boys."

We turned around. She was naked. The moonlight turned her saffron skin to bronze. Her brown nipples shown dark and her public bush was a stark, shining black.

I don't know about Michael, but I was fully erect before she had gotten all of the way in. I was overjoyed that I had sat already.

We sat there, equidistant in that round hot tub, not quite out of touching distance from each other, and talked quietly some more about the production that we'd seen that night. About the Cyrano we were rehearsing.

Cindy's small breasts floated on the water, the thick nipples poking through the foam.

When the talk finally ran silent, Cindy sat up on the edge of the tub, moonlight burnishing her glistening skin. "You guys find me... attractive. Don't you?"

Michael and looked at each other, nodded, and then looked away.

"Well," Cindy continued, voice low and throaty, "you are both very attractive too. And so here is my proposal: I want to fuck you both. At the same time."

I could hear Michael cough in shock, even as her suggestion, which shouldn't have been a surprise but for some reason was, made my jaw drop.

Grinning at our reactions, Cindy continued, "But only if it's both of you. If either or both of you are uncomfortable with this, and want to leave, I'll totally understand, and that we'll be the last time we'll ever talk about it, but I'll expect the other one to leave as well."

We sat there for a good thirty seconds, listening to the water and the bubbles.

I looked over at Michael. "I'm game," I said, though I was sure that I didn't know what I was agreeing to.

Michael looked at me, then at Cindy, and then back at me. He stood. His cock was half-mast in the hot water. "I can't," he whispered.

"Michael," said Cindy, but he was already out of the tub, off the deck, and out of the house.

I've always wondered if he bothered to get dressed on his half-mile walk back to his place.

I looked back at Cindy, who hadn't moved, whose flesh seemed to be blossoming with goosepimples. "Cindy," I said, "please — "

She shook her head. "No, Ken, I meant it, I can't fuck just one of you, I — "

"How about I don't fuck you?" I whined. "How about I just eat you?"

Cindy didn't say yes. She didn't say no. Her face was wide and uncertain, but her legs parted and I took that for my answer.

That set up a pattern that lasted through the rest of that summer. We never fucked, but whenever Cindy was feeling horny, she would spread her legs, or lift her skirt — or, once, during the interminable last act of Cyrano, her nun's habit — and, like the lapdog that I'd become, I would pleasure her with my mouth.

I know that I must have gotten off somehow during these exchanges, though I'm pretty sure it was by my own hand most of the time.

Michael and Cindy and I stopped hanging out all of the time. The Antonia from River Shakes started appearing during their dark nights. "The best man won," I toasted him.

He grinned and nodded to where Cindy was talking with her friend Jen and with Antonia — whose actual name was Sally. "You and Cindy?" he asked.

I shook my head.

That night, Cindy took me back to her hot tub again — and as I brought her off, she moaned out the name Jen.

When I asked her about that, Cindy blanched. Tearfully, she admitted that she was in love with her strawberry blonde friend, and had been for a while.

"I like guys too," she said, searching my face.

"I don't really care who you like," I said, "if you don't love me."

"I'm sorry, Ken. I do like you." Reaching between us, she grabbed my cock. "You want to fuck me, tonight?"

It wasn't much of a fuck. And it didn't change how she felt about me. But I'd be lying if I said I didn't feel much happier afterward.

* *Allison's stories are told in the Juliet Takes Flight tales. And yes: there will be a FFM ménage story coming in that series soon!*

Dear Reader,

Thanks so much for reading my first collection featuring groups of friends becoming... more than friendly!

See below for more of my stories — including a sneak preview of the next story of Lea and her boys' adventures.

I write these stories because I really enjoy telling them, both the sexy and the not-so-sexy bits. If you've gotten this far, I hope that you've enjoyed reading it too. Either way, I'd love to hear from you. If you want to talk to me about my stories — if you have comments or questions or just want to grumble or gush — wow, I would sure love to hear what you have to say! You can email me at kdwest@stillpointdigital.com, or you can go to my blog (kdwestwrites.wordpress.com) and send me a comment.

You can also connect with me on Twitter (@ KDWestWrites), Facebook, Pinterest, Google+, Tumblr, or even LinkedIn.

If you do, I'll send you a short story for free by way of thanks. I really look forward to hearing from you.

I'd also really love it if you clicked on one of the links below; let people know what you think of what you've read!

There are more stories coming out in this series; I'm coming out with a new one every month. Keep an eye on my blog or on the Stillpoint/Eros site for news.

Until next time!

K.D. West

Also by K. D. West
print books, ebooks and audiobooks:

Collections:
Four Erotic Tales: Letters to Allison (M/F)
Three for Three: A Trio of Friendly MMF Ménage Tales... Plus!
(M/M/F)
Juliet Takes Flight:
Juliet Takes Stage (M/F)
Juliet Takes Off (M/F)
Juliet Takes Her Leave (M/F)
Juliet Takes a Chance (F/F)
Erotic Tales – Letters to Allison:
Thing of Beauty (M/F)
Bridget: Virgin Knot (M/F)
The Big Easy (M/F)
Veronica (M/F)
Friendly Ménage Tales:
Truth and Games (M/M/F)
Over the Top (M/M/F, M/F)
The Visitor (M/M/F)
The Visitor Comes Home (M/M/F)
COMING SOON!
The Visitor Returns (F/M/M)
The Visitor Entertains (F/M/M)
The Visitor Takes a Trip (F/M/M)
The Visitor Has Company (F/M/M, F/F/M)
Meredith (M/F)
Allison (M/F, M/F/F)
Juliet Takes the Floor (M/F/F)
Juliet Takes Charge (M/F, F/F, M/F/F)
Opening the Door (M/F, M/F/F)
The Trouble with Triplets (M/M/F, M/F/F)

(Go to the next page to get a sneak peek at the next story in this series!

The Visitor Comes Home

A sneak preview at the next story of Lea and her boys' adventures!

Lea was back in a bathroom airplane; her legs were down this time, and her panties were up; she was done using the facilities, and masturbation was the last thing on her mind — and the last thing that her body could handle.

Sean and Andy had made very sure that she'd had all that she could handle over the last three days. And nights.

Well, more than she could handle, which she wouldn't have thought possible. She wouldn't be walking straight for days. Probably wouldn't be able to touch herself for weeks. Well. Till the next day, anyway. Well. Okay. Maybe until that night. If she were careful.

Not that she would be complaining any time soon.

But what she wasn't sure how to handle was how to explain any or all of this to her best friend and roommate, Kirsten — Sean's sister. Lea couldn't think of a good way to approach the fact that not only had Lea finally, finally bedded Kirsten's older brother, whom Lea'd crushed on and lusted after since the two women were still in college, but that they'd frolicked with Sean's roommate. Who, like Sean, was a tall, broad-shouldered, Southern firefighter. A wet dream on legs.

And that was quite outside the difficulty of letting Lea's best friend know that she would be leaving San Francisco at the end of the month, leaving Kirsten without a roommate.

It was overwhelming to feel so excited and satisfied at the same time as Lea felt nervous and sore.

The bell rang and the captain's voice rang out. "We've got some turbulence ahead. Please take your seats and buckle your seat belts. We'll try to keep this as smooth and as entertaining as possible."

Thanks, thought Lea. Will you come home with me?

When Lea texted Landed! from the airport and didn't get a text back, she figured that Kirsten was at work; the Union Square store looked askance at pulling out your phone on the sales floor. Still, it would have been nice.

So Lea sent the same text to Sean and Andy and was gratified to receive great miss u from Andy and WHEN ARE YOU COMING BACK???? from Sean. She was grinning from her head to her aching hamstrings as she boarded the BART train and texted back Can't wait to come back there and burn down the REST of Dixie!

Her two Georgia boys informed her that would never happen, not even if she brought Sherman and his whole army.

She informed them — as her bus approached her stop — that the only army she planned on encountering when she came back to Atlanta was the two of them, and she had every hope that the South would rise again. And again.

Which they solemnly promised her it would.

Backpack on her back, Lea was giggling — giggling! — as she made her way up to her floor, fished out her keys, and threw open the door to the crowded one-bedroom that she shared with Kirsten.

— The Visitor Comes Home

About K.D. West

The author of the Erotic Tales: Letters to Allison and Juliet Takes Flight story cycles as well as the up-coming novel A Joy Forever: An Erotic Education, K.D. West is a teacher, writer and performer living in a small suburb of a big city:

> Not a huge amount to say — I'm an author of steamy stories who happens to be a teacher; these things don't mix well in public, so I tend to be fairly quiet about real life in my blogging. I am, however, interested in all sorts of things -- books, writing, theater, mythology, and, obviously, erotica! I'm a huge reader of genre fiction — mostly mysteries and fantasy, but also science fiction and historical romance.

West has written two intertwined series involving a young woman and her older lover (the *Juliet Takes Flight* and *Erotic Tales: Letters to Allison* stories) and a series of stories about friends discovering that they can become much more *(Friendly Ménage Tales)*. Also on the way: an erotic paranormal/urban fantasy novel involving a long lost friend coming all-but-literally back from the dead, and showing a happily married couple just what they'd been missing.

Stillpoint Digital Press

Stillpoint Digital Press creates fine ebook, audiobook, and print editions in genres from fiction to literary nonfiction, from memoir to poetry.

In addition to publishing, Stillpoint provides editing and other publishing services to independent publishers, aiming to give a human face to digital publishing, offering a full range of editorial services, from editing, layout and ebook conversion to distribution and marketing.

For more about Stillpoint Digital Press and its books and services, visit us on the web at http://stillpointdigitalpress.com

READ MORE STILLPOINT TITLES:

STILLPOINT/ROMANCE
The Mercenary Major: A Regency Romance by Kate Moore
Sweet Bargain: A Regency Romance by Kate Moore
Sexy Lexy: A Contemporary Romance by Kate Moore

STILLPOINT/MYSTERY
Death in a Fair Place: A Ben Felkin Mystery by W.L. Taylor
Dread in a Fair Place: A Ben Felkin Mystery by W.L. Taylor

STILLPOINT/THOUGHT
Myths to Live By by Joseph Campbell
A Joseph Campbell Companion: Reflections on the Art of Living
by Joseph Campbell
Gods & Games: Toward a New Theology of Play by David L. Miller
Excursions to the Far Side of the Mind: A Book of Memes by Howard Rheingold

STILLPOINT/VERSE
Easing into Dark by Jaqueline Kudler
Sacred Precinct by Jaqueline Kudler
Practice by Dan Belmm
Space/Gap/Interval/Distance by Judy Halebsky
The Stranger Dissolves by Christina Downing

STILLPOINT/MEMORY
Sail Away: Journeys of a Merchant Seaman by Jack Beritzhoff
Pasta in My Bra: a Saga of Cerebral Palsy by Nicole Sykes

AND MORE!
stillpointdigitalpress.com

www.ingramcontent.com/pod-product-compliance
Lightning Source LLC
Chambersburg PA
CBHW020549130626
46552CB00007B/2832